The French Detective

a collection of short stories

Erwin Hargrove

To Paul

For your enjoyment

Erwin

Text © 2017 Erwin Hargrove. All rights reserved.

Cover illustrations:
detective © 2017 Panptys/Shutterstock.com
Paris night © 2017 ducu59us/Shutterstock.com

All rights reserved. No part of this book may be reproduced or transmitted in any form or by any means, electronic or mechanical, including photocopying and recording, or by any information storage and retrieval system, without permission in writing from the publisher

ISBN 978-0-9971561-6-4 paperback
978-0-9971561-7-1 epub
978-0-9971561-8-8 mobi

CONTENTS

PREFACE

DEATH IN ENGLAND   1

MURDER OF A NASTY MAN   31

DEATH OF AN ACTRESS   67

A MYSTERIOUS MURDER   111

WITHOUT A GUN   139

MURDER IN THE OPERA   159

PREFACE

Inspector Jules Lavin's physical appearance is not described in any of these stories. The reader may ask, 'what does he look like? Does he have distinguishing features or mannerisms?" He does not and, after living with him for some time, I think that I know the reason. He is an 'everyman' sort of person because this enables him to be a good detective. He does not want his appearance or personality to get in the way of his inquiries. He prefers to ask questions and listen carefully to the answers. A more pronounced personality might confuse or intimidate those with whom he talks, whether witnesses or suspects.

Lavin is of middle height. He is solidly built, neither lean or fat. He has light brown hair with a touch of gray and his complexion is somewhat pink. He loves to smile and laugh with his friends and family but he does not smile much when he is at work, except out of politeness. He can be irritable in private but he does not show it nor does he ever get angry. You would not pick him out of a crowd. But for this very reason he may carry out his inquiries without appearing to threaten anyone. He is a perfect man to be a detective.

He is very intelligent without being an intellectual. He is analytical and empirical at the same time. He throws up hypotheses and tests them with the incomplete evidence available. One can follow inquiries in the stories and see where he is going but often at the end of the chain of clues he will receive an insight that will solve the crime. Thus, though he is highly rational he often relies on his intuition at the end of the day.

DEATH IN ENGLAND

Chapter 1

It was a beautiful July morning. Four travelers joined many others to board a large ship in Calais on the northern coast of France. They were to go to Brighton on the southern coast of England, arriving in the late afternoon. The ship had ample seating, lounges, restaurants, even a movie theater. The four sat together for the most part but also wandered around the ship individually. They talked, read, napped, and generally relaxed. They were on their way to a commiseration. Great Britain had voted to leave the European Community, and the four travelers had worked hard for the "remain" cause in collaboration with the English colleagues they were to join. The purpose of the meeting was to ask what might be done to plan for an exit with as many bonds as possible.

Georges Beaumont, a veteran member of the French Senate, who had served in a number of ministries in the past, was their initial convener and informal leader. A journalist, Danielle Morel, had earlier written many stories on England and Europe. She had also worked in the combat zones of Iraq and Afghanistan.

Beaumont was a conservative politician, and she was sympathetic to the socialists, but they both wanted the UK in Europe.

Alain Lecoq was a young, politically promising deputy in the French parliament, a man of the political center. He was a dedicated European in his politics, more so than most of his fellow politicians. The nonpolitical member of the group was Adolphe Joubert, an investment banker.

Beaumont was handsome with silver hair and an angular face. He had the reputation of a ladies' man, but no one held it against him. He and his wife had recently divorced, and he was often seen in Paris restaurants with actresses and other interesting looking women. He liked women as such and was not a sexual predator. Danielle was forty or so, still very good looking, with auburn hair and large green eyes.

Lecoq was small, and he spoke and moved quickly with energy. Finally, Joubert was sixty or so, somewhat round with a quick smile and penetrating eyes. They were a compatible group, comfortable with each other, and conversation flowed easily and quickly.

The trip of several hours was very pleasant. The boat was like a floating city.

Danielle wrote on her laptop, Joubert read business journals, Lecoq read a book on English politics, and Beaumont studied passengers, walked around, and often talked with people whether he knew them or not. He liked to strike up conversations and was a good listener as well as conversationalist.

The blue blur of the English coast eventually came into view, and they rose to depart. Brighton was a festive city, and it was pleasant to leave the ship in the bright sunshine and find the car and driver at the docks waiting to drive them to Dorset. They were to stay for the weekend at the home of Guy Craig, a minister in the British government, a long time Conservative politician.

Craig had initiated the Anglo-French group as one of a series of actions in behalf of Britain remaining in Europe. He and his colleagues had done the work in the UK, and the French participants had provided factual ammunition for the cause. The other members of the English group were John Post, a Tory MP, journalist and prolific writer on political and economic subjects, and Roger Walker, an economist. They had all gathered and done their work at Breakwater, Craig's home on the coast of Dorset.

The traveling group arrived at Breakwater in the late afternoon to find their English counterparts waiting in a large lounge with windows open to the sea. Greetings were warm and genuine, and conversation continued through drinks and dinner. It was a large house with bedrooms for the French guests. The two Englishmen were staying at an inn in town, The Three Feathers.

They convened for breakfast in the morning around a long dining table next to a side board filled with hot dishes of eggs, ham, muffins, and hot and cold cereals. People helped themselves, and two maids provided coffee, tea, and anything else needed. The conversation picked up from the previous night as knives and forks clattered, when Danielle suddenly said in a clear voice that all heard, "Where is Georges?"

No one had noticed that he was not there. There was silence. Finally Guy said that he would go find him. "Perhaps he is walking out to see the sea."

He walked around outside and then walked upstairs and knocked on Beaumont's door. When no one answered, he entered the room to see that the blinds were still drawn, and Beaumont was evidently sleeping in bed. He was reluctant to wake him, although it was almost ten o'clock, and approached the bed, calling Beaumont's name softly. This brought no results, and as he got closer to the bed, he did not like what he saw. Beaumont's face was contorted as if he were in pain. He shook him slightly by the shoulder, and the body was stiff and unyielding. Craig had been in combat and knew a dead man when he saw him. He quickly left, went to his own room to call a doctor, and then went downstairs to inform the others. It was distressing for all of them, and they went to the lounge to wait for the doctor's arrival.

Dr. Hubert Ross arrived and examined Beaumont carefully. Those waiting expected him to tell them of a heart attack in the night. Instead he spoke quietly. "This man was poisoned sometime in the past twenty-four hours. I cannot be more specific without an autopsy. I have called the local police and they have alerted Scotland Yard. We should hear from them soon."

Chapter 2

Inspector Hugo Fry of Scotland Yard arrived at the house by noon, accompanied by other detectives. He examined the body and Beaumont's room and then ordered an autopsy to be done as soon as possible. He then spoke to the assembled party in the lounge.

"I cannot tell you much until we have the results of the autopsy. This does not appear to be a suicide, because there is no poison in the room. We have to assume that a murder has taken place. We will want to talk with each of you as well as the house staff. I know that all of you had planned to return to London and Paris tomorrow, and we will do our best to accommodate you. However, we need to investigate the murder first. Sergeant Murdoch will collect your names and addresses so that we may stay in touch with you throughout the inquiry. I have called the Paris police, and they are sending a man who is expected to arrive tonight."

With that, Fry set up a command post in the library and began to interview all present one by one. He kept a careful record for the French policeman. Craig was the first to be interviewed. He explained to Fry who the group was and why they were meeting. They were all friends, he said, and he could not imagine a murderer among them.

"Did all of you go to bed at the same time?" Fry asked.

"Yes, more or less. Post and Walker left for the inn about ten o'clock, and the rest drifted up to bed slowly after that. Beaumont and I stayed downstairs a few minutes to finish our drinks and talk politics but not for very long. My room is on the ground floor in the back of the house, and I said good night to him at the stairway."

"Did he appear well?"

"Yes. He was in an excellent mood and enjoying himself thoroughly. He was a bon vivant who enjoyed life."

"Were there any disagreements or tensions among you during the evening?"

"No. Our talk was constructive about how to best modify what we thought to be a mistake in the British referendum."

"Have you known M. Beaumont long?"

"Only for a few years. We have both been active in Anglo-French groups. My parents took holidays in France when I was a boy so I am a Francophile. When the question of British "Brexit" began to loom it seemed natural for us to do something together, so we formed our little group."

Fry talked with the two Englishmen, Post and Walker, and learned that they had spent the night at the inn and come to 'Breakwater' for breakfast. They had little to tell him. He then decided to talk with the French guests as a group and let his French counterpart talk with them individually, probably the next day.

The French guests were more visibly upset than the English. Beaumont was their colleague and friend. Lacoq had known him for several years. Danielle had written about him. Joubert had only known him slightly before Beaumont had recruited him for the group, but he admired his political perceptions and his intelligence. They had all gone up to bed at the same time, leaving Craig and Beaumont behind, but Lecoq said that his room was next to Beaumont's, and he heard him enter it not long after he had gone up. No one had heard anything in the night.

Inspector Jules Lavin of the Sureté arrived late in the afternoon. He had flown to Brighton and been driven to Dorset. He introduced himself to Hugo Fry and Guy Craig. He and Fry were not acquainted, but each knew the other favorably by reputation. Fry spoke somewhat adequate French, and Lavin's English was tentative and hopeful. But they could get their meanings across. Craig's excellent French filled the gaps at times. Fry asked Lavin to speak with each of the French people and said that they would then meet and make a plan for an investigation.

Chapter 3

Lavin began with Danielle Morel. She wanted to get back to work in Paris, because her editor was pressing her. She described the trip and the evening in straight forward fashion. Beaumont had not been agitated as far as she could see.

"What did you think of the Senator?" Lavin asked.

"He was a principled politician, a conservative who had lost his chance to be President of France when Sarkozy became President. Yet he had considerable influence in government as seen in his leadership of the current parliamentary investigation of the Pakistani bank accused of corruption."

"I understand that he was active with the ladies?"

"Oh yes. He was a terrible womanizer but not a predator. He never attacked women to my knowledge. But he moved from one lover to another. His wife tolerated him for twenty years, but she has recently divorced him."

"Did his affairs lead to any scandals or conflicts, with husbands, for example?"

"I have been abroad a good deal, so I would not necessarily know. I think that an aggrieved husband sued him a few years ago, but it was settled out of court. Most of his women friends were young and unmarried."

"Tell me about the Pakistani bank."

"It is the Banque Commercial in its French name. The owners are in Karachi. They have been accused, but not yet charged, of money laundering, in particular of funds earned from the sale of opium in Afghanistan. This is said to have benefitted the Taliban, which harvests and sells the opium. That is the question that Beaumont's committee, working with the authorities, had begun to investigate."

Lavin thanked her and said that she would be able to go home soon. He then talked with Alain Lecoq. They covered the same ground about the trip and Beaumont. Le Coq was skeptical that Beaumont's committee would move now that he was gone. He had been the animating force, and the other members had other interests. However, he thought that the French police would stay on the case. Lavin knew of the investigation and resolved to learn more about it.

Adolphe Joubert had been recruited to the group by Beaumont, because he was much involved in trade between the UK and the continent. He was conversant with politics but knew little about Beaumont personally. The interview was brief.

Lavin and Fry then sat down to work out their plans. Fry's team would comb the crime scene, interview the house staff and talk more with the English participants. Lavin would return to France and begin to open up whatever he could about Beaumont's work and life, as well as keep touch with the other French people there. Each would inform the other of any discoveries.

Lavin knew from working in the past with English detectives that each nationality had a different mode of detecting. The English stayed close to the evidence and worked inductively from one clue to another, broadening the search as they went. He and other French detectives collected personal histories of those involved and eventually developed hypotheses to guide their search for clues. The English and French would meet at the same point in the end, but they often got there differently.

His first two areas of inquiry were Beaumont's womanizing and the affair of the bank. He began with the womanizing and called Christine Beaumont, the Senator's former wife, to ask if he might talk with her. They met the next day at her elegant apartment on the edge of the Bois de Bologne.

Christine Beaumont received Lavin graciously in her apartment. She told him that she was shaken by her former husband's death. "We knew each other for thirty years and were married for twenty. He was easy to love because of his great charm, and he was, in fact, a very kind man who cared about others."

"May I ask why you divorced him?"

"I put up with his woman chasing for years, and it wasn't that so much. But I became a figure of ridicule among my friends and in the press, because I tolerated it so long. I was seen as an enabler. There is greater tolerance for womanizing in France than in 'Anglo-Saxon' countries, but less so than in the past because of a few well-publicized cases."

Lavin took this at face value.

"He seems to have been a well-liked man. Why would anyone wish to kill him? Did he have any enemies?"

"He had political opponents, but most of them liked him. There was an outraged husband and another father of a young woman who were both very angry with him in the past. The husband was angry because Georges approached his wife at a party and asked her to have lunch with him. He was even more angry, because she accepted and met Georges the next week."

"What happened then?"

"The husband stormed into George's office, rushed past his secretary, and grabbed George's necktie as if to strangle him. He shouted in the poor man's face to leave his wife alone. It was very embarrassing for Georges."

"Was that the end of the matter?"

"Oh yes. But I remember another case of an angry father who threatened to sue Georges for romancing his eighteen year old daughter, who should have known better."

"How was that settled?"

"Georges lawyer talked with the father's lawyer, and Georges wrote a letter of apology to the daughter and the father, saying that his interest in the girl was strictly 'paternal.' No one swallowed that, especially the girl, but the father was mollified. Georges had to promise never to approach her again."

"How you feel about all this?"

"I was more amused than anything. George's carelessness would get him into comical scrapes, but he always managed to escape."

"He seemed to be a 'devil may care' man, but he was a serious politician?"

"Yes. He idealized women and was very much an idealist in politics. He believed strongly in his brand of conservative politics, which required government to be limited, fair, and honest. He was not a friend of business particularly. He saw government as a public trust. He had been a Gaullist and was still one in a sense."

"Can you give me any examples of his political idealism?"

"He was an advocate for greater opportunity for Algerian and Moroccan migrants to France, past and present. Many young men are confined to the banalieus in urban districts without adequate schooling and employment opportunities. He worked with many politicians on the left for this cause, something his own cohorts tried to ignore."

"What can you tell about his investigation of the Pakistani bank?"

"It was in the early stages. The staff was still doing research, and they were compiling a list of witnesses. He thought they were a bunch of crooks making money off the Taliban and helping them at the same time."

She gave Lavin the names of Beaumont's closest friends, mostly politicians, and promised to help him as he proceeded.

Lavin was not quite sure how to proceed on the womanizing front and decided that Beaumont's lawyer was the best way in. He found Marcel Bonin in a chamber in the third floor of a stone office building near the old French Opera. The firm was known for its representation of celebrities, including notable politicians and government officials.

"I understand that you represented M.Beaumont in several instances. Can you tell me about those cases?"

Bonin smiled wryly. "I oversaw his personal financial affairs, but you surely are referring to other aspects of his personal life, particularly the case of the angry husband, or perhaps the matter of the furious father?"

"Were there other cases as well?"

"Oh yes. He loved beautiful women of any age. I managed to appease the husband and father by apologies and promises. Complaints from husbands and lovers were frequent. He could not help himself. There may be men who are still angry with him, but I do not know of a recent case."

"Did he ever force himself on a woman?"

"No. He was a lover, not a predator. In every other respect, he was a good man."

"Do you know of any threats against him, any enemies?"

"No. He was well liked."

Lavin was not completely satisfied on the womanizing front and called the aggrieved father whose name Christine Beaumont had given him.

Gustave Lacoste held forth in an office on the Champs Elysee. His offices occupied one floor behind a glass door with the name of the business, an import-export firm, in large golden letters. He was a bulky man with a red complexion. Lavin suspected high blood pressure and a temper.

"Beaumont was a scoundrel," he told Lavin. "He charmed my daughter and pretended a paternal interest, and he fooled her."

"Do you think that he meant to seduce her? She was very young."

"I am sure of it, but he never got the chance."

"He did not seem to be that unprincipled. What would you have done if he had seduced her?"

"I would have killed him."

"Do you know of any threats of that kind against him?"

"No, because we kept the affair as private as possible. I heard of one other case of a German woman diplomat whose husband made threats against him."

Lacoste did not know the names of either the man or his wife. Lavin thanked him and then called a friend at the Quai de Orsay, the Foreign Office, and asked for help. His friend said that he would look into it and called a week later with a brief story.

"The woman's name is Hilda Jurgens. She and Beaumont met at a conference in Geneva. She is ordinarily based in Berlin. Her husband Basil, is a banker in Berlin. One does not know if Beaumont seduced her, but the two of them stayed in Geneva for several days after the conference ended. She claimed that she was vacationing."

"What happened then?"

"Basil decided to go to Geneva to see her – a kind of surprise – and there she was with Beaumont, not in bed, but close to it. She went back to Berlin with Basil, and we do not know the end of that story, but Basil wrote the President of France, raising hell."

"Did he threaten Beaumont?"

"Yes, he did. He said that he would kill him if he approached Hilda again, and according to reports that we have about Basil, he might have done it."

"Do you know if Beaumont and Hilda ever met again?"

"They were both at an EU conference last month. We know, because our fear of a scandal made us keep tabs on both of them. They stayed in different hotels, but we know no more than that."

Lavin could not quite see how Beaumont could have been killed by Jurgens in England, but he did think about the boat. He called Inspector Hugo Fry and asked about the results of the autopsy.

"I was going to call you today". We just got the results. Beaumont was poisoned with Methanol which is slow-acting within a twelve to twenty-four-hour period. It is a fermented grain used for paint remover. That explains why he showed no symptoms and died in the night."

"I wonder if he could have received the poison before he left France."

They agreed that was possible. Lavin would look into it. Neither man mentioned the boat as a possibility, but Lavin later thought of it. He had to find out what Beaumont had done the morning before he sailed. He learned that he had not gone to his office and had told his secretary that he would go directly to the ship from home. So he went to see the porter at Beaumont's apartment.

"Did you see M. Beaumont leave the other day on his trip to England?"

"Yes, sir, He left about ten in the morning."

"Was anyone with him?"

"No, sir, but a young lady left his apartment about six in the morning. We have a video of her departure."

Lavin looked at the video. The woman was clearly French, young, leggy, and, Lavin had to admit, sexy. But how find out who she was? He called a friend of Beaumonts who was likely to know the women whom Beaumont enjoyed, but no luck. She was a new face and body. He called the head of a model agency and sent her the video in hopes of identification. Then he called a movie producer who specialized in films with leggy young women, but no luck again. Paris was full of good looking, leggy young women.

He kept this unresolved problem in his mind and turned to the investigation of the Pakistani bank.

Chapter 4

Lavin had no difficulty contacting Marie-France Laurent, the chief of staff of the Parliamentary Committee looking into the business of the Al Habib Banque Ltd. The bank's headquarters was in Kirachi, Pakistan, with branches throughout south Asia, Western Europe, the United Kingdom, and New York and San Francisco. It had been founded by Fahad Darrani, a Pakistani citizen of Pashtun descent.

"What do you know about Darani?" Lavin asked.

"He is a Pashtun with close ties to Pashtun warlords in Afghanistan, some of whom are close to the Taliban. He is a former member of the ISI, the Pakistan army intelligence organization, which has protected the Taliban, we believe. He is very hostile to India, as is the ISI. None of this is illegal. But we believe that he has been laundering money for the Taliban from the sale of heroin grown in Afghanistan. Of course, we must prove it. Our actuaries have been at work tracking deposits and expenditures, and we are getting warm. We would like to get evidence from bank employees, but no luck so far. We thought that we had a man in Islamabad who had agreed to talk, but he was beaten so badly that he had to be hospitalized. We are still waiting to talk with him."

"Have you interviewed bank officials in Paris and other European capitals?"

"Yes, but they play dumb, claiming that their business is here in Europe. An examination of their accounts confirms this fact. If there is laundered money in the bank system, we cannot find it here."

"So the money from heroin sales is somehow disguised in Pakistan itself?"

"We think so, primarily through shell companies that are vehicles through which to make deposits in the bank itself. The funds can then travel throughout the bank wherever it works."

"Does the government of Pakistan cooperate with your inquiry?"

"The straight answer is no. We think that the bank is protected at the highest levels of government."

"How can you proceed with such an obstacle?"

"We have been able to show that some of the shell companies are sham. We do not need to be in Pakistan to prove that. We have tracked their histories. Of course, we are not close enough to learn how the heroin is sold and then put into those companies, but we are working on it."

"What is the market for heroin, and who are the buyers?"

"The market is worldwide. The buyers are Asians, Latin Americans, Europeans, anyone in the retail drug trade. We know who they are, but it is not easy to catch them. They are secretive, armed, and dangerous."

"Did M. Beaumont ever receive any threats from Pakistani sources related to the work of the committee?"

"Yes. He received a number of anonymous letters warning him to back off, but he was not the kind of man to pay any attention."

"Did he consider having a bodyguard for protection?"

"Several people suggested that to him, but he was the kind of man who thought that he was invulnerable. You may have seen signs of this in his private life." She said this with a smile.

Lavin chuckled. But he was not in a good humor, because it was not clear what he should do next. He called Hugo Fry to report on his work and find out what Fry had achieved. The answer was very little. The Dorset house staff were clean, as were the two Englishmen who had slept in the inn. Neither Post nor Walker had any past involvement with Beaumont nor any relations with Pakistani banks. Craig and Beaumont were old friends.

The two detectives discussed the possibility that Beaumont could have been poisoned before or during the trip. Lavin's story of the disappearing woman was a loose end. They then discussed the possibility of poisoning on the boat. Lavin said that he would talk again with the members of the French group about Beaumont's actions on the boat. They remembered that they had sat together most of the time, but as she was talking, Danielle Morel remembered seeing Beaumont talking with a woman in separate seats some distance from the others. He seemed to be enjoying himself, and she had thought nothing of it. She remembered the woman to be good looking with long black hair. Danielle, having spent much time in South

Asia, did not think that the woman was European.

This report excited Hugo Fry. "A Pakistani woman fitting this general description has come to our attention recently. M16 has been interested in her. She has diplomatic status and has worked in their London embassy. Word has come through that she is an agent of ISI. M16 wants to know why she is here in England. It may mean nothing, but they like to keep track of ISI agents."

The woman's name was Suzanne Mohamed. She was half French and had been in the Pakistan diplomatic corps for ten years. M16 thought that she was a secret agent working undercover, although their knowledge went no further than that.

Fry and Lavin went to work at each end to see if she had purchased a ticket to travel from Calais to Brighton. Her name did not come up, but she could have bought a ticket under another name. They obtained a photograph of her and showed it to Danielle, who easily identified her. The picture showed her to be extremely good looking, thus verifying Beaumont's taste in women.

Every effort to find her failed. She had left her London apartment. The Embassy of Pakistan said that she was traveling in Europe. She had not been reassigned to return home. There was no trace of her. The Pakistan Foreign Service reported, after a delay, that she had resigned from the diplomatic corps to return to private life. The detectives expected that she might show up later on the staff of the bank in Karachi, but they had absolutely nothing on her. If she did surface later, they could pursue the case, but the cooperation of the authorities in Pakistan would be uncertain.

They had probably solved the crime, but the criminal had escaped. And yet, Lavin had a long memory.

MURDER OF A NASTY MAN

Chapter 1

Jacques Lebeau was not a happy man, nor was he a nice one. He was murdered at age 70. Why so late in his life? Jules Lavin thought that perhaps an old enemy had found him, or maybe Lebeau was conflict with someone recently. How had they gotten to him? He was living in a retirement home in the country. This was Lavin's difficulty. There were so many potential suspects at Parc Manor, and lots of suspects outside, especially in Paris. The autopsy revealed that Lebeau had died from a pistol shot to his head.

Lavin was a specialist in murder of all kinds, but he had never confronted a "rooming house" murder with so many suspects. Fortunately for him, the Parc Manor was in the small town on the Normandy coast where his daughter Sophie and her family lived. He looked forward to visits with his grandchildren while he interviewed suspects.

Lebeau was a writer, a general critic of books, theater, films, politicians, and anyone or anything in the life of France that invited his biting criticism. He had never married and seemed to have no family. He had entered Parc Manor because of his asthma, and had wished to distance himself from people who annoyed him in Paris. He had continued to write for newspapers and magazines. People wanted to read him, even if they disliked what he wrote. He had a long career as a journalist and critic, but little was known of his personal history or private life. He had lived in Paris and had known many people but had kept only a small circle of friends, if one could call them friends.

Lavin and his wife, Sylvine, drove from Paris to Veule-les-Roses on a beautiful afternoon. They were to stay with Sophie and her husband Anton while the detective opened his investigation. He had not been called to the scene when the body was discovered and would have to depend on the local police for the important details. Lebeau had been a sufficiently important person for the Sureté to send their best detective.

Lavin and Sylvine arrived at Sophie's home about noon. She had canceled sessions of her psychotherapy practice so that she could be there to welcome her parents. Sophie and Anton lived in a rambling cottage just outside the town. Anton was a lawyer with a practice in the region, and they would see him at dinner along with Adele and Jules, who were then at school.

After a brief lunch, Lavin drove two miles along the Atlantic coast to Parc Manor. It was a comfortable looking brick building far enough from the water to avoid strong winds but close enough for a lovely view. He asked himself if the rooms in the back were less expensive, but the colorful gardens there quieted that thought. Some people preferred flowers to sea breezes. The front hall was small, but one could see a spacious lounge on the left and a handsome dining room on the other side. A few people were lingering at their tables.

He approached the front desk and introduced himself. It happened that the manager of Parc Manor, Bertrand Bonnet was standing there. He was a "hotelier" if Lavin had ever seen one: courteous, smooth, efficient and discreet. Lavin was in Bonnet's office before he could say a word.

"This is a terrible thing Inspector," said Bonnet. "People leave us all the time, but nature takes them and does so quietly. I do not like to see Parc Manor in the Paris newspapers, and I suppose that we will be in the obituaries when they come out. I understand that you must investigate this horrible event, Inspector, but I urge you to do so as circumspectly as you can so as not to disquiet our residents. As you can imagine, a good many are upset, not because they cared for M. Lebeau but because of the crime."

"I will do what I can M. Bonnet, but I will need to talk with many people, including your staff."

Bonnet gave a sour expression and replied that he understood, when in fact he did not and wanted the whole situation to go away. At Lavin's request, he called the local Inspector of Police, Vincent Fournier, and handed the telephone to Lavin so that they might talk.

A brief conversation ensued, and Fournier said that he would be there in fifteen minutes. In the meantime, Bonnet walked Lavin through the building – library, lounges, back terrace, kitchen, a small bar, and rooms in the two wings of three floors each. There was a small infirmary with nurses on duty. Lebeau's room had been cordoned off by the police.

Lavin asked Bonnet if Lebeau often had visitors. The question induced a blank look.

"Visitors must sign a guest book by the front door. You can check, but I do not know of any. M. Lebeau would go to Paris on occasion with a driver to see a play or talk with an editor, I believe, but those trips were few in the two years that he lived at Parc Manor."

Fournier was a veteran local policeman experienced with burglary, car thefts, and petty stealing but not murder. He was deferential to Lavin, knowing him by reputation. He had a jovial round face and a big smile.

"I regret your having to come here M. Lavin, but we need you. I will help in any way that I can."

Lavin thanked him and suggested that they look at Bonnet's room.

They rode the elevator to the third floor and walked down the hall past ten doors to an apartment on the front with an ocean view. One could see the Atlantic breakers crashing into the rocks below. The apartment had a bedroom, living room, study, and bath. The study was lined with filled bookshelves, a large desk with papers on it, and a telephone. A file cabinet stood beside the desk. A lap-top computer was on the desk. There were no photographs in the apartment, but the walls were covered with copies of paintings by French impressionists. The cabinet over the sink in the bathroom contained one bottle of pills and two inhalers. Lavin asked Bonnet if a doctor was in residence, and when the answer was yes, he asked to see the doctor as soon as possible.

Fournier had brought two policemen, who searched the room thoroughly, the closets and bureaus, and the desk. There was no gun. The bullet that had killed Lebeau was from a small caliber pistol, strong enough to kill him.

It was not long before Dr. Arlette David appeared. She was a healthy looking middle-aged woman, who, he later learned, was a native of the town.

She told Lavin that she had treated Lebeau for asthma.

"His asthma was chronic but episodic. He responded well to the medicine, and his inhalers, one stronger than the other for a heavy bout, worked pretty well. The asthma was probably going to get worse as he grew older, but one cannot be certain."

"What can you tell me about him other than that?" Lavin asked.

"He was a difficult patient, who questioned me at every step and continually asked me about my medical training. He was nasty with the nurses who gave him his medicine and the women on the floor who kept his room up. I had the clear impression that he was not friendly with his neighbors. I noticed that he usually ate alone in the dining room and never attended the social hour before dinner."

The autopsy had been conducted by a doctor from the Department, the regional government. Lavin asked Fournier to get him the autopsy report. He then asked the doctor and Bonnet to leave, and he and Fournier began to read the papers on the desk.

They made two piles and each took a stack. There were bills, personal letters, newspapers and magazine articles, some by Lebeau and some by others, and a few typescripts presumably written by the dead man but lacking his name. Lavin assumed they were unpublished. Most letters were routine correspondence about the publication of Lebeau's work. He then looked at the manuscripts. They were critical essays of a professional kind.

The letters about articles that would be published were familiar copy editing questions. One editor thought that Lebeau's criticism of an author in a book review was "unfair," but the critic insisted and got his way, as the published review revealed. Lavin made a note of the book's author. There was one note to the editor of a popular magazine in which Lebeau promised a story that would be a marvelous "expose" of "salacious sexual life" in an unnamed institution. The editor wanted it as soon as possible.

Lavin looked again through the unpublished items. Most were book reviews, and there were a few highly critical profiles of public figures, including a prominent politician. This was standard fare for Lebeau, but Lavin did not see grounds for murder, thinking in common sense terms. He thanked Fournier and arranged to see him the next day at his office.

Then he wrote down possibilities for interviews in Paris and elsewhere if necessary. He would talk with editors. He would interview authors whom Lebeau had attacked. Finally, he would try to find friends or at least acquaintances who had known the murdered man over the years. Before he left the manor, he asked Bonnet to give him names of all the current residents and those who had left within the last year, unless they had gone to their reward. He also asked for the names of all the staff at the manor, their positions, and their dates of service.

Then he went home to see his grandchildren. This was a happy time. Adele was ten and as pretty as her mother, and her grandmother for that matter. She had an infectious smile and always laughed at her grandfather's jokes. Jules, named for his grandfather, was twelve and very serious, a new Boy Scout who was fascinated with nature, particularly beavers. He told his namesake all about how beavers created their dams and homes. Sophie finally had to ask him to stop and wash for dinner. They ate a delicious meal of roasted duck, washed down with red wine, around a circular table in the kitchen. Then the children got ready for bed and the family settled down to discuss the crime.

Sophie had some patients at Parc Manor and was familiar with the place. "It is for the 'haute bourgeoise' and a few pretenders to old aristocratic titles," she said. "It is expensive, and the service is excellent. It is not an easy place to manage, because the residents are very demanding. The manager, M. Bonnet, spends a good deal of time answering complaints and smoothing out conflicts."

Her father asked her who was important in the management in addition to Bonnet.

"The head Housekeeper, Md. Arseneau, is a power in her own right. She oversees the kitchen and all housekeeping. Claude Roux is in charge of the grounds, and he and Md. Arseneau have a continuous, but quiet, war over responsibility for the gardens. He sees them as his fief, but she claims a concern on behalf of the residents. He wins, but she meddles."

Most of the residents frequented the village shops and many owned cars and took trips on their own. The place was frequently filled with visitors, families and friends, especially on weekends. Parc Manor was more like a residential hotel than a nursing home. There were some very old people who lived in one wing on one floor, but they also got around with help when they felt like it.

Lavin asked if there were any well-known people in residence.

"The Countess d'Arbison Deschamps, an elegant woman, lives there. She is about seventy. Her son and his family live in the family home nearby. She evidently prefers to live alone rather than with the family, but they visit her often, and she goes to see them. There are a number of retired business people, who are surely known in their work. A former actress, who I think was once well known, Charlotte Daubry, has not lost her charms, for she holds 'court' among men in the dining room every night."

After a good night's sleep, Lavin went along to Fournier's headquarters. The autopsy report was straightforward. Lebeau had died from a gunshot to the temple. The time of death was estimated to be between one and four a.m.

Lebeau usually ate alone, but on the previous night he had dined with four people at the invitation of the Countess Deschamps. She had told him that she and others wanted to hear his ideas about an upcoming French national election. Lebeau was a conservative as was the countess. The two others at dinner were Pierre Lefevre, a retired Catholic priest and Charlotte Daubry, the actress. Lavin made appointments to see each in turn in a private room in the building.

Lefevre was easily seventy-five. He was a Jesuit, who had taught at various universities. His family was wealthy and paid for his residence. He had a long, angular face and very alert eyes. He smiled at Lavin.

"I hardly knew Labeau, Inspector. I taught philosophy and am interested in political theory and politics. I thought M. Lebeau might be interesting, even though my sympathies are on the Left."

They discussed Lefevre's career. He had taught in Britain, the United States, and Germany, in addition to France. He only knew Lebeau by reputation and did not know much about him. He would occasionally visit him to talk about politics.

Charlotte Daubry knew Lebeau and did not like him. He had been critical of some of her films, and she was not a forgiving person. But the countess had invited her, and she had not wished to be impolite.

Lavin was looking for clues about Lebeau, any clues at all. He asked about Lebeau's life in Paris.

"He kept apart from ordinary social life," said Charlotte Daubry. "I would see him at the theater, at large receptions, occasionally in the Luxemberg Gardens by himself. He had one friend, a professor of French Literature, Rene Dupont. I would see them together in restaurants. Dupont was said to be Lebeau's only friend."

Lavin made a note to contact Dupont. He then had to decide whom else he would interview at Parc Manor. There were one hundred and twenty-five residents, mostly women except for twenty men. He decided to begin with the countess and called for an appointment, to which she agreed.

The Countess d'Arbison Deschamps was elegant. She was still beautiful at seventy, with auburn hair, deep blue eyes, and high cheekbones. Her figure was slim and lithe. Any man would find her still attractive. Lavin eased into the interview by asking her how she liked Parc Manor.

She told him that she liked it well enough. Her life was comfortable. She had tired of Paris society but still spent a month in her Paris apartment in the spring and the fall. She wanted to keep up with old friends, of whom there were fewer every year. She also liked being close to her only child, a son, and his wife and her three grandchildren. The Count had died six years ago, and she still missed him. He had preferred country life to Paris, so they had enjoyed this area for many years. A few of her friends had nearby country homes.

As for Lebeau, she said, "He was an interesting man but a misanthrope. He didn't like people, and this was clear in his writing. He could be entertaining in person because of his sardonic wit. No one was safe. I enjoyed his writing about French politics. He thought that most politicians were phony posers. He had no positive beliefs so far as I could tell. I share his contempt for our politics. I am an old fashioned "royalist," meaning that I would like to see a restoration of authority in some form."

Lavin asked if she knew whether Lebeau had any friends.

She thought a minute. "I think he had a mistress for some years, but then they parted. Her name was Miriam Stewart. She was English, but I think she lived in Paris.

"I knew Lebeau for many years, Inspector, but never well. He used to attend the salon discussions that my husband, M. the Count, would hold. We were patrons of the arts. Lebeau was always aloof, even distant. One had the impression that he did not like people."

Lavin thanked her and left. He asked Bonnet if he might then talk with the chef and the staff of waiters. Seven people were duly brought into the lounge.

The chef, Md. Marie Morel resented this inquiry. She purported to know perfectly about her domain. She had been in charge for twenty years. In fact, the interviews yielded nothing. The waiters went home at night and arrived early in the morning, and no one knew anything about the movements of M. Lebeau on the night in question. He usually ate alone, and since they took turns serving him, none had anything to say about him except that he had no courtesies.

Lavin then asked to speak with Md. Arsenau, the housekeeper, and her house staff of ten women. She was even more formidable than Md. Morel, the chef. The idea of a murder in "her" house appalled her as if it were an affront to her personally. She admitted that Labeau was a difficult person to look after, and the housemaids all nodded yes, except for one young woman who volunteered that he had been nice to her. The faces of the others indicated that they saw her as inexperienced and naïve. The Infirmary was open at night, and one housemaid was stationed on each floor to respond to emergencies. Md. Morel insisted that no one could get in the building at night. A doorkeeper guarded the front door, and the side and back doors were securely locked.

Then came Claude Roux, the groundskeeper. Lavin wanted to know if there was a way to get into the building through a window, especially on the first floor.

Roux said that it was possible, but there were no signs of broken locks or window panes. His house was secure, he announced.

Inspector Fournier had been asked to do his best to find criminal histories of all Parc Manor employees. Most were from the local area. With that, Lavin decided to return to Paris.

Chapter 2

Lavin and Sylvine said good bye to Sophie and drove back to their apartment in the Marais district. He went to his office and made several telephone calls. Miriam Stewart's name was in the book, and she answered her telephone.

"My goodness, Inspector. I have not seen or spoken to Jacques in ten years. I was one of the few people who could abide him. He had a soft spot that I found appealing, but it grew harder over the years, and I finally cast him off." She said the last phrase humorously.

Lavin met with Miriam in a small café near her apartment She was a fashion designer who had lived in Paris for years. Her French husband had died prematurely, and she had taken up with Lebeau. She was perhaps in her early sixties, good looking, with an extra flourish to her manner.

"Jacques was a very insecure man," she said. "I think that his mother was distant and the father was too often away. He essentially raised himself and trusted no one. Rene Dupont and I were the only people he trusted and to whom he would reveal himself. We gave him the emotional security he lacked."

"Why would anyone want to kill him?"

"People whom he offended might want to do it on the spur of the moment, because his words were wounding. You would have too many suspects in that case. He was not involved in the lives of others, as far as I could see, to create any murderous passions."

Rene Dupont, in his rooms in the Sorbonne, agreed with Miriam Stewart. "I got along with Lebeau because of a common interest in French literature, particularly theater. We often went to plays together. He did not mix with theatrical people and did not even know the playwrights and actors whom he would tear apart in his reviews."

Dupont did not know of any long-term feuds with theater people. Lebeau had been too remote to have personal enemies. He was also too good a critic. His reviews of novels and plays were not uniformly hostile, which was why they were read.

"He did have a long running feud with the novelist Roger Gautier," said Dupont. "They may have met, but the feud was entirely on paper, in newspapers and magazines. Gautier is a writer of the Left and Lebeau pilloried his characters as lacking authenticity, as only vehicles for political ideology. Gauthier is very sensitive to criticism. He once slapped a critic in the face in a Paris restaurant. But nothing came of it."

"Did they ever meet?"

"I cannot say for sure, but Jacques would not have gone beyond an introduction and brief conversation with people he did not like or did not approve of."

The case looked more and more as if the killer had been inside the manor as a matter of course or had entered the manor and hidden until night. When Lavin met Gautier, he thought that the novelist was not capable of the latter feat. He had uncertain balance and moved only with a metal walker. He remained seated as Lavin was ushered into his apartment by a servant. He was tall man with a craggy face and wild hair.

"I did not kill him, Inspector, but I could have, with my bare hands, in a fit of rage, had I been the man I used to be."

They had a long talk about Lebeau and his life in Paris.

"He was detested, but my life as a novelist tells me that people do not kill for intellectual reasons. The motive must be emotional."

Lavin's next stop was the editor of the magazine to whom Lebeau had promised the "salacious" piece. The magazine was about current affairs with a lively sample of news and gossip about personalities in the news. The editor was Simon Lemaire, a veteran journalist. Lavin explained his mission, which was based on the correspondence between Lebeau and Lemaire about the promised story.

"He did not tell much about the piece, Inspector," said Lemaire, "but I had the impression that the institution to which he referred was probably Parc Manor."

"Why do you say that?"

"It seemed awfully close to home, and he said that he had acquired a good deal of rich detail. He had not been close to any other institution in the recent past. For example, if he were talking about the Comedie Francaise or the

Opera, he would have to have been around to do the digging for a story. One could have just come to him as a gift, but even so, he was a good reporter and investigator. He was also very sensitive to libel law, because he had legally libeled so many people through criticism."

"Did the promised story have a theme?"

"Sex, I think. It would an expose. I doubt that he was preoccupied with ordinary crime. It was to be about 'misdeeds.'"

After their conversation, Lavin went home for lunch and to talk with Sylvanie. They had light crepes with fruit and a glass of white wine. He confessed that he did not have a single useful lead.

"You are not going to find the killer in Paris," Sylvanie said. "If he or she is here, or anywhere in France, you have no way to find them. We must go back to Veule-les-Roses. You will find the murderer there by searching. Even if the killer is not there, I would guess that someone there knows who it is."

So they went back to Sophie's happily.

Chapter 3

Once Lavin and Sylvanie had settled in, Lavin called Fournier. It was late afternoon, and they met in a small café near the water. Lavin watched the surf and hoped that the surges would incite his imagination. Detecting relied on evidence, but imagination was required to find it and then to know what to make of it.

Fournier had nothing negative to report about any of the staff except to say that he had learned that Bonnet had been involved with a number of women over the years, often in the hotels where he had worked. He was a lover, if not a womanizer. It was not clear what to make of this, so they set it aside and continued their discussion.

It did not seem likely that an intruder had been able to break into the manor at night. There was no evidence of a break-in. Only the most professional burglar would not have left a trace. Someone could have entered during the day and hidden until nightfall. But where would they hide without being discovered by a staff worker? Still, it seemed possible. Yet Lavin had no candidate. They parted, agreeing to talk again.

It seemed, therefore, that the killer lived at the Manor. Lavin's interviews with the staff had stirred no ripples. He would have to look more carefully at the residents. They looked at the list of 125 occupants. Counting those who were in the Infirmary on the night in question and those on the floor who needed help moving around, one hundred were left. This was a needle in a haystack problem.

Lavin sent the names to the appropriate bureau in the Sureté for criminal records. Word came back the next day that one retired businessman in the manor had once been arrested and tried in court for fraud but had been not been convicted. It was a financial matter having nothing to do with literary life.

Lavin decided that he needed gossip. This was a good way to learn about people and their connections. He called Charlotte Daubry and asked if she would have lunch with him the next day. He suggested a restaurant in the country away from both the Manor and the village. He would pick her up at the Manor gate at noon.

She agreed and was there, wearing a bright red frock that did justice to her figure.

"This is exciting. I don't get taken to lunch often. But I assume it is business. Still, I am happy to help with a little sleuthing."

"I have resorted to sleuthing, Madam, because a detective needs solid evidence, and I have almost none. So I need to search for clues, tangible or intangible, anything that will help. I think that you are an observant person, and as an actress, an intuitive one. I hope that you can describe the 'folkways' of the Manor. I need to know the cast of characters more fully."

After they had settled over red checkercloth tablecloths in a corner of the restaurant, Lavin asked the actress for the main themes of gossip in recent weeks or days.

"The most juicy gossip has been why Adelaide Gerard left us so suddenly. She had been here several years. She was about seventy, a former dancer who had arthritis, which was not disabling. She vanished overnight."

"Do you know why she left and where she went?"

"I do not know why, but I received a short note from her the other day. She is living in a retirement home in Paris."

So, back to Paris and a visit to the 'Hostel pour les Anciennes' near the Bois de Boulange. He had called in advance, and Mme. Gerard had agreeably said that she would be happy to see him. Her apartment was richly furnished and was filled with photographs of ballet dancers in action as well as single pictures of Mme. Gerard at center stage in performance.

"You understand why I am here," he told her. "I need to know as much as possible about Parc Manor because I have few clues to M. Lebeau's murder."

Mme. Gerard was tall and thin and moved with the quiet elegance of a dancer. Her face would have been clearly seen from the audience, large eyes, a curved jaw, and black hair. She listened and then thought a moment.

"I suppose you want to know why I left Parc Manor so abruptly. It is a personal matter. But perhaps I can help you. I was romantically involved with M. Bonnet for a time. You may know that he has a history of such affairs. It was sex more than love. He is a seductive lover. But he threw me over, so I left."

"Did he leave you for someone at the manor?"

"It was the countess. I am more attractive than she, but she is wealthy and could perhaps give him a more secure financial future than I could."

"Did he tell you that she was your successor?"

"No, but one could see it in their relations, even in the full view of others."

"Did anyone else see this or comment on it?"

"One night, as I was leaving the dining room, M. Lebeau asked me how I liked sleeping alone. I just looked at him. He had a cynical look on his face. I made no comment and left the room. I had decided to leave Parc Manor, and this confirmed my decision. I was not going to be the subject of gossip."

"Did the countess know about your affair with M. Bonnet?"

"I don't know. He may have told her."

Lavin had an idea as they were talking. Had Lebeau known about the affair of Bonnet and the countess? He might have detected it in their behavior. This could be the story he was promising to the magazine, but, as Rene Dupont had told him, Lebeau was careful to avoid the charge of libel in his writing.

Lavin suddenly remembered the housemaid who had said that Lebeau was nice to her when he had talked with Md. Arseneau and her staff. He called Sylvanie to tell her that he was going back to the manor for a short time, perhaps overnight, and called Sophie to tell her. Then he drove back to the coast, arriving in the early afternoon.

Lavin asked Md. Arseneau if he might talk with that particular housemaid, alone. She agreed reluctantly. In a few minutes, Regina Duval came to him in the room he was using. She was clearly very nervous.

"Don't be nervous, my dear. You are not in trouble. I am just seeking some facts. I remember that you told me that M. Lebeau was always nice to you. Is that correct?"

"Yes sir. He was very polite."

"Did he ever ask you to do anything especially?"

"I would bring his mail from his box, and sometimes he would ask to see a newspaper from the lounge after it had just arrived. I would deliver notes to others in the manor on occasion."

"Were these notes addressed to the management or to other residents?"

"To both, but I can't remember who."

Lavin let this pass. "Did he ever ask you about the movements of people, for example, as residents visited other residents?"

Regina had calmed down, but her nervousness returned. "I never spied on anyone."

"I understand, dear, but did he ask you about who visited whom on occasion, as a matter of gossip?"

"Yes, we talked about that."

"What did you report to him?"

"Well, two men regularly visited the countess. One was Father Lefevre, and the other was M. Bonnet."

"Did M. Bonnet come at a regular time?"

"I noticed it only when I was on duty at night."

"Were M. Lebeau and the countess on the same floor?"

"Yes, but they were several apartments apart."

Lavin thanked her for being helpful and reassured her that she was not in trouble. He then left the Manor and went to Sophie's for the night, calling Sylvanie to tell her that he thought that he had solved the case but still had more work to do.

That night after dinner and after the children had gone to bed, he told Sophie and Anton what he had learned. "I know that Bonnet and the countess were a romantic couple. Mme. Gerard and Regina Duval have told me that. It is likely that this was the story that Lebeau had promised M. Lemaire for his magazine. It seems unlikely that he would have identified them by name, but he would have written it in such a way that those who knew them would know."

Lavin then asked,

"If this is so how might either the countess or Bonnet know that they had been discovered, and would they care?"

Anton, the lawyer, said, "If they had known, they would have surely cared. A manager is not supposed to sleep with the residents. The countess would have been embarrassed to be sleeping with a mere employee, and she would not have wanted her son and his family to know such things."

Sophie then asked, "How did they find out that Lebeau knew?"

Lavin made a guess. "I expect he told the countess in order to make fun of her, just as he had done with Charlotte Daubry." And Anton then asked,

"You may have a motive for murder, but do you have proof?"

"No," said Lavin. "I must somehow get it out of Bonnet and the countess."

He went to bed, turning it all over in his head. But the case was nearly solved, and he slept well.

The next morning, Lavin called the countess and asked if he might visit her in her apartment at 10 o'clock. She agreed and had set tea things out before he arrived.

"Madame, I have an unpleasant task this morning. I am going to have to charge M. Bonnet with the murder of Jacques Lebeau."

The countess appeared startled but said nothing.

"I believe that he knew what M. Lebeau knew of the affair that you and M. Bonnet were carrying on and feared that Lebeau would write about it."

She still said nothing.

"May I take it that you do not deny the affair?"

Finally, she asked, "Surely you are not listening to cheap gossip?"

"I do know for a fact Madame, and I would never rely on rumor."

"Even so, my private life is a matter for me alone. It is none of your business."

"It is, when one is trying to find a murderer."

This blunt remark seemed to take her back. "What do you mean?"

"I suggest that M. Bonnet killed Jacques Lebeau to prevent the publication of a story that would damage you both. And I also suggest that he learned about what Lebeau knew from you."

"This is outrageous. Are you suggesting that I was an accomplice to murder?"

"Not at this point, Madame. I will talk with M. Bonnet."

He abruptly left the countess and went to Bonnet's office. When he arrived, he walked in without knocking.

Bonnet was just putting down the telephone. His hands were shaking.

"That was the countess," Lavin asked?

Bonnet said nothing and just looked at him.

"Must I do the talking?" Lavin asked.

"You have no proof that we were entangled. You have no proof about the murder. You are just looking blindly for something you cannot find."

"I have good evidence of the affair. I think that you will tell me about the crime, because you wish to protect the countess. She can afford expensive defense attorneys for you."

"What if I am innocent, and the countess shot Lebeau?"

"I do not think that she would do that. She is not a murderer except at second hand. I suggest that you conspired with her, and that you shot him."

Bonnet said nothing at first and then demanded, "Bring charges against me. They will not stand."

Lavin immediately returned to the countess.

"Bonnet informed me that you shot Lebeau."

"That is not what he just told me on the telephone.

"He is not being honest with you. He told me that you were very worried about a scandal, not only about you, but for your family, so you obtained the pistol and shot Lebeau."

"That is not true. I have never fired a gun and would not know how, nor do know how to get one. Bonnet is a liar. Lebeau did tell me that he knew about our affair and warned me that was not the last that I would hear about it. He was a very nasty man. Bonnet and I talked about it, and Bonnet said that he would settle the matter. That was the last I heard of it until the murder itself. I am innocent."

Lavin thought that the countess was telling the truth. She was not a murderer, but the prosecutor would have to decide. He called Inspector Fournier and directed him to arrest Bonnet immediately. Then he went back to Sophie to say goodbye and returned to Paris. He looked forward to a glass of red wine and a good dinner with Sylvanie.

DEATH OF AN ACTRESS

Chapter 1

She had been shot in the back of her head, but one could not see the hole, because her beautiful auburn hair had been carefully laid over it. She was lying on the sofa as if sleeping and was as beautiful in death as in life. Lily Martine, an actress of stage and film, had been, at young middle age, in the prime of her career. Her manager had called several times. She was usually out and about, but no one had seen her. Imagine the shock when they rushed in to see that she was dead rather than ill or asleep.

Inspector Jules Lavin, of the Sureté, was an expert at murder. He had unraveled the most complex crimes. He was forty-five, his hair was still coal black. He had an angular face with high cheek bones. His dark blue eyes were almost black, and he could talk with someone without any hint of his own thoughts. He was taciturn, given to asking questions while withholding comment. His lieutenants were never sure what he was thinking, and he often surprised them with his directions.

Lavin examined Lily carefully and directed a careful search of the luxurious apartment. She lived alone. The doctor estimated that she had died between ten and twelve the previous night. It was curious that she had been shot in the back of the head and then carefully put down as if sleeping.

Her manager, Giles Francois, told Lavin that Lily had no children. Her closest relative was a sister in Lyons from whom she was estranged. She had been married three times, and two of her former husbands were alive and in France. Francois had been her manager from her early years as an actress, and he appeared to know more about Lily than anyone in sight.

"What was she like?" Lavin asked.

"She was a very fine actress, and she knew it. She would not waste her time on mediocre productions. The very best directors wanted to work with her. She spoke English well. Her mother was English, and her father was French. Her sister, Marguerite, was younger and much less cosmopolitan than Lily. Marguerite has a grown daughter who has MS. Lily has tried to help them financially, but Marguerite does not think that she has done enough and broke off relations some time back. Lily was a good person who helped young actresses in their careers and was kind to all who worked with her. She had one weakness. She was a terrible judge of men."

"In what way?"

"Neither of her first two husbands were her equals as good people. Her first husband, Georges Dupuis, was a handsome young actor, much in love with himself, and a constant womanizer. She sent him off after a year or two. Her second husband, Ralph Gibbs, was an English director, who drew marvelous performances from her. But he was an alcoholic who destroyed his own career. He eventually drank himself to death. Her third husband was Pierre Picard, a movie producer. He provided stability and money, although she did not need it. They were married for ten years and separated but never divorced. I think they are friendly, but I know nothing about their relationship."

"Did she have lovers?"

"If so, one never knew. Her best friend in the theater was an English actor, Robert Graves. They acted together on the stage and in movies, but I do not think they were lovers. He seemed devoted to his wife Catherine, who died a few years ago."

"Did you manage her contracts and finances?"

"Yes, with the help of her long-time lawyer, Claude Lesage."

Lavin decided that he should talk with Lesage and called for an appointment. The lawyer's office gave an atmosphere of learning and gravity, with law books lining the shelves and rich leather furniture.

Lesage matched the setting in his demeanor. Right away he said, "I was very fond of Lily. Not only was she talented, but she was smart and easy to work with."

Lavin asked if he had handled her divorces.

"Yes, I did. She did not suffer financially from either of them. She has no financial tie with Picard."

"Was she well to do?"

"Indeed, she was, and she expanded her fortune well through investments. She has been able to live a good life, travel, and have a home in the country as well as a fine apartment in Paris."

"Who will inherit her money?"

"Her sister and niece will benefit most, but they do not know it. She intended to leave a good sum of money to a foundation to provide limited support for aspiring actors but was reconsidering that decision because of negative reports about the foundation's activities. There were stories of arbitrary awards. She was a member of the board and was making inquiries."

Lavin thanked him and went home for lunch. He and Sylvine had been married for twenty years, and they discussed his cases, because she had learned to be a good detective just from listening to him and making suggestions. She had good intuitions and often opened blind spots for him. She was blondish, a bit younger, and very pretty. He could not imagine life without her. Their daughter, Sophie, lived in the country with her husband and two children.

As they enjoyed their crepes, Jules mused aloud. "This could be a crime of passion but not on the spur of the moment. It was almost like an execution in which she was shot deliberately. The killer did not hold her in order to slander her, because there were no burn marks of a close-range shot on her neck or head. It appears that the killer waited until her back was turned and then fired. This suggests that the killer knew her. Perhaps the killer did not wish to fire at her front or could not do so. She was very beautiful and was arranged on the couch to show that. So if this was a crime of passion, it was a planned and calculated one."

"Perhaps so," Sylvine said, "but acquaintance and passion are different. The killer seems to have come to murder her."

He agreed. He would have to talk with Lily's sister, explore relations with the foundation, and interview her legal husband, Pierre Picard. He decided to talk with Picard first and called him the next day. The story of Lily's death was in the newspapers that morning.

Picard's office was in a large glass building in the collection of tall buildings on the Champs-Élysées. He was seventy or thereabouts, a tall, elegant man who had produced films of artistic merit for many years. Lily had acted in several of them. He did not look well to the Inspector. His eyes were dark and his face drawn. The news had evidently hit him hard.

"Please sit down, Inspector. I may have trouble gathering my thoughts this afternoon. This has been a terrible shock. Lily was so vital and alive. One cannot believe that she is gone."

Lavin began gently. "I understand that Lily was a wonderful person as well as a very talented one. Can you tell me how long you knew her?"

"I knew her for many years, since she was a promising young actress. She was in one of my films, ironically a murder mystery, when she was in her twenties. I did not know her well then but had always wanted her in my films, if possible. Her second husband, Robert Gibbs, was a brilliant director who got wonderful performances from her in both French and English films. He was a tragic figure in his weakness for drink, and toward the end his talent dried up, and he no longer worked. Lily stayed with him until he died, and that was when I came to know her well. She turned to me for comfort. Lily was a lonely person in her talent. She was such a good actress, nurturing her career over everything else, that she had only a few friends. I think that she was devoted to Gibbs, not only because he did so much for her artistically, but because she cared for him. I think that she had a weakness for injured people like Gibbs or her first husband, George Dupuis."

"Then why did she turn to you?"

"Because I am like the Rock of Gibralter. I gave her love and support that she had never had. She and her sister grew up in a troubled family. Their parents were actors of limited range who lived a transient life moving from one theater company to another with little economic security. I gather that her father was an affectionate parent when he was home. Her mother was talented chiefly in her beauty, but that will only take one so far in the theater. The girls loved their parents, I think, but were unhappy in their restless way of life."

"Were both girls actresses?"

"Yes, but Marguerite was less successful. She married early and had a daughter who developed MS. She has spent much of her time and energy looking after Dominique. Her husband was a lawyer with a promising career, but he died of an embolism when he was thirty-five, and Marguerite has had to struggle financially. He left a small estate, and she has worked as a literary agent with some success."

Lavin and Picard agreed to keep in touch, and Lavin called Lily's sister, Marguerite, in Lyon. She told him that she would be in Paris for the funeral in two days and agreed that they

Death of an Actress

would talk afterwards at her hotel. Her daughter Dominique would be with her.

The funeral was in a church in St. Germain des Pres. An Archbishop officiated with an elaborate mass. Giles Francois chose the pallbearers, since Lily had designated none, nor had she left any instructions about her funeral. The church was packed with theatrical people and worshipful admirers, many of whom could not get in because of the limited seating. The service was on both radio and television and was something of a national event. The Archbishop eulogized Lily's talent and stressed her character as a good Catholic and a friend to all. There was much weeping, especially among those outside who listened to the piped radio broadcast.

Lavin went from the service to the Pavillion Hotel to talk with Marguerite. She was a good-looking woman somewhat younger than her sister, but she appeared to Lavin to be worn down by life. Dominique was in her twenties and was also pretty. She walked well with Canadian crutches. When they were seated in the parlor of the bedroom suite, Lavin asked when Marguerite and Dominique had last seen Lily and how she had seemed at that time.

"We have not seen her since the summer," her sister responded. "She dropped in to see us on her way to her country home near Rousillon in Provence."

"Did you see her often?"

"No. Our relations were frosty. We lived in different worlds and had trouble connecting."

"Were you close once?"

"Yes, we were, as two sisters close in age with difficult parents. We had to look out for each other."

"What happened to separate you?"

"She became a celebrity with little time for us, and I married, moved to Lyon, and gave up acting. In later years, I have spent much time with Dominique."

"Was there antagonism between you and your sister?"

Marguerite looked at him abruptly, with sharp eyes, but he did not speak and waited for her reply.

"I regretted having forsaken acting, although I loved my husband, but I missed the theater. I suppose I was jealous. Lily's life was so busy that she had little time for anyone else except Ralph Gibbs, who also directed her movies. She wasted her time on her drunken, dying husband, so we saw little of her. After he died, she tried to make up, but I was not interested."

"What about her third husband, Pierre Picard?"

"He is a very nice man who encouraged us to reconcile, but we somehow never got around to it."

"What was your relationship with Lily, Dominique?"

"I liked her. She was always nice to me. But I saw her less often than I would have liked."

Marguerite's face was red. She did not like her daughter's comment, as if it were her fault that they had seen little of Lily.

Lavin let the moment pass. "Did Lily have any enemies?"

"None that I know of. There was one actress, who I think was Italian, against whom she contended for parts, and there were rumors of 'bad blood.' But I know nothing about it."

"Did you feel that your sister should have done more to help Dominique?"

Marguerite did not like the question and looked away in annoyance. "That is a private matter. Why should I talk with you about it?"

"You need not. I am just trying to understand Lily."

"She could have done more. Dominique has had good medical care, but we lack income at times. I make a living as a literary agent, but it is stop and go. I would have appreciated more help."

"Did you ever ask her to help?"

"Of course not. I am a proud person. She could have seen that we were struggling and done more for us."

Lavin wondered whether such a proud person would ever have accepted help from a sister she disliked. He also sensed a mood of jealously. He felt that he had learned enough and paid his respects and left. It was not his place to tell them of Lily's will. Evidently the lawyer had not yet talked with them.

Lavin asked Giles Francois if Robert Graves, Lily's English actor friend, had attended the funeral and found Graves still at his hotel. They met in the lounge and spoke in French. He asked Graves about his history with Lily.

"We were in one of her early pictures together. We were not paired romantically in the picture as was the case later, especially in English pictures. We were cast well together. I was the aloof Briton, and she was the alluring but difficult to capture French woman. We became good friends in time."

"Why, do you think?"

"She was half-English and liked us. I was never sure why. I think that she liked our respect for privacy. She was very private person. But that does not explain our friendship. She and my wife, Catherine, became very close and affectionate with each other. Catherine was plagued with bouts of cancer on and off, and Lily was always concerned about her. She and I became friends in our concern for Catherine, and after Catherine died five years ago, the friendship grew even stronger. Of course, we continued to act together on occasion."

"Not a romantic relationship?"

"No. We were drawn to each other's attractiveness but more out of a mutual respect for our talents than love."

"Did she have lovers?"

"I doubt it very much. She would have never been unfaithful to Pierre."

"Why do you think they separated?"

"She needed space. He gave her comfort and security, but she needed to be alone as well. They continued to be very good friends and never divorced. She was not the kind of person to take serial lovers. Commitment was too important to her."

"Did she have any enemies?"

"Rivals, yes. Many actresses were jealous of her, but I cannot imagine that she had enemies. She never acted to hurt anyone."

The Inspector then went to see Md. Anne Lefevre, the executive director of the Foundation for the Theater. She was tall, handsome, and theatrical. She did not seem particularly sad about Lily's death. He presumed that she did not yet know about Lily's bequest to the foundation.

He decided not to waste time with routine questions.

"I understand that Ms. Martine was not happy with some of the grants the foundation has made to aspiring actors"

Her eyes became dark, and she stared at him with quiet anger.

"Who told you this? It is not true. Lily was an active board member and never raised any questions. You have been misinformed."

"I think not. She thought that too few grants went to Arab or African aspirants, despite their numbers in the profession."

"There have been grants to such people, but too few of them are qualified."

"Are you sure that she voiced no complaints?"

"Of course. Why do you come in here to libel us and Lily?"

He detected a bias in her use of the word 'qualified' but saw no point in going on, so he did not apologize but simply took his leave."

Chapter 2

Lavin had learned something about Lily but not much else. None of the people to whom he had talked would seem to be murderers. Her sister would benefit from her death but she was ignorant of the fact. The Foundation may have hoped that it would benefit, but murder did not seem plausible. The killer was a professional. He or she had come armed to kill and had done so smoothly. It was likely that the gun had a silencer, which was also professional. He had to discover something about Lily's life that was beneath the surface.

Lavin returned to the lawyer and asked if Lily had an archive of personal and professional correspondence. Lesage answered that the archive was under his supervision and stored in a depository that he used for his own documents. He had no objection to Lavin examining it.

Lavin went home for the day. Sylvine had prepared a veal cutlet and a mushroom soufflé, which they savored with good red wine. He told her that he was out of leads.

"You may find something from her personal life," she said. "But she lived a circumspect life. You must also look elsewhere. Did she have political commitments? Did she contribute to any causes?"

If this was possible, the archive would seem to be the best place to look. He arrived at the solid brass doors early the next morning just as they opened. The material was catalogued, and he asked to have it brought to him. He was given a room with a large table and a computer, which he had learned to use belatedly in his career. The professional catalogues appeared to be about business matters for the most part although there was correspondence with producers, directors, and other actors. He decided to look at her personal correspondence first.

He found a series of letters in which Lily had refused to act with an American without giving any reason. She told producers that she preferred other Americans, whom she named. Evidently, she got her way, as she had appeared in movies with other Americans. She gave no reasons for her rejection. Lavin then found one cross-reference of the American's name with letters to and from Lily's friend and fellow actress, also an American, Caroline Page. They had been friends for years, and Lavin had to sift through many letters before he found promising material.

Caroline and Lily would not act with the American in question, because he had a reputation for sexually exploiting young actresses with promises of parts in his movies and then breaking his promises. Caroline knew personally of one instance in which the actor had raped a young woman. The poor girl would not press charges for fear of the effect on her career. Lily had gotten to know her while acting in America and had taken up Caroline's argument without success. The two women had given serious thought to exposing the actor themselves, but they could do nothing without permission of the victim.

Finally, after the young woman had established herself as an actor, she agreed to talk with the police. Naturally the actor denied all, and the police were reluctant to get into it without other similar cases. However, they were waiting for him to try again and warned him to that effect. The man in question thus knew the part played by Caroline and Lily, but this did not seem ground for murder, especially of Lily, who had entered the story late.

    Lavin dove back into the archive to see if he could find any political themes. Lily had not been active in politics. She had thrown her personal and financial support to the exposure of French priests accused of molesting juveniles and had written a number of bishops expressing her strong views. Again, murder did not seem plausible, especially since the offenders were in jail.

    On another day, he discovered that Lily had sent money to a Syrian actress friend to help her move, with her children, to France. Lily had also spoken out against terrorism in the wake of the 2015 terrorist attacks in Paris and Brussels and had marched with President Francois Hollande along the Champs-Élysées after the attacks. Photographs showed her clearly in the front line near the President. A number of French celebrities had been publicly vocal at the time, and Lavin could not immediately fathom why Lily might have been a terrorist target.

Besides, the nature of the crime did not fit the profile of a terrorist.

He was at loose ends again. Lily's murder must have been due to things in her personal life, but what?

Chapter 3

Lavin continued to comb Lily's letters for clues. One name appeared often in the years between 1980 and 2010, that of Peter Dumont. The letters were between affectionate friends. Dumont.

Dumont was a Paris theatrical producer, who had sponsored some of Lily's stage plays. The letters were filled with descriptions of everyday doings but were laden with affection. For example, Dumont wrote at Christmas, 1985: "We go to the country for the holiday, but I will miss talking with you, especially at this time of the year when one wishes to be near loved ones. I will call you when we return in hopes that we can have lunch. All my love, Peter."

Lily's reply was sent to his office in Paris: "I will miss you, my dear. Please call when you return. We will have a break for a few days from filming, and I will spend Christmas eve with Maurice and Eve and the day with my good friends Richard Graves and his wife Priscilla, who are in Paris. How wonderful it would be to be together at Christmas with you some year. Much love, Lily."

The letters disclosed that Peter's marriage was not happy. His wife, Cecile, had been an actress of some success, but her career had withered in her later years, and she blamed Peter for not doing enough to help her. At times, she even accused him of sabotaging her work. Their daughter, Ami, who was a novelist, was close to her father and took his side with her mother. She knew about her father's friendship with Lily and had eaten with them often. They had kept this from Cecile.

This was the tenor of the letters over the years, but in 2000, there was an abrupt and sad change. Peter had a stroke and was confined to his Paris apartment for the most part. Ami would take him to parks in his wheel chair to see Lily. He was able to write and talk on the telephone with Lily, although they had to be careful that Cecile was out of the apartment when they talked. Ami was the go-between. She would mail Peter's letters to Lily and pick up her letters at his office. He continued to work on a limited scale.

Death of an Actress

The relationship between Peter and Lily began as her second husband, Ralph Gibbs, was in its last years with his alcoholism. After his death, Peter suggested gently to Lily that he was more than ready to leave Cecile and marry her. She put him off for some time and finally told him that she could not marry him, because he was married. Her first marriage had been annulled, and she was free to marry in the eyes of the church, but he was not. Her Catholic faith was too important to her. Marrying a divorced man would bar her from Holy Communion.

Cecile did not know that Peter and Lily were friends. She had met Lily in theatrical social circles and no more. After Peter's stroke, Cecile would take vacations by herself or with friends, leaving Peter with a nurse and Ami. This gave Lily and Peter the opportunity to meet, usually in out of the way spots, and always with the help of Ami.

One day, on return from a trip, Cecile was told by a friend that she had seen Peter, Cecile and Ami lunching in a little restaurant in the country outside Paris. Cecile assumed the worst and created a scene with husband and daughter in which she charged both of them with treachery against her. Protestations of old friendship did not do any good. Cecile ordered Peter to break off with Lily and wrote a scathing letter to Lily.

The luncheon visits stopped, but the letters continued. Ami would bring Lily's letters to Peter for him to read and then take them away so Cecile would not see them. However, she carelessly left a letter behind, and Cecile found it. She was so furious that she threatened to sue Lily, although the grounds were not clear.

Lavin asked Lesage if he knew of the affair, and the lawyer said that he had received a letter from Cecile's lawyer about the grievance, but neither lawyer could see any grounds for a lawsuit, and they so informed Cecile. Cecile had declared war on her husband and daughter by this time and, in response, Peter moved in with Ami, leaving his wife alone. This led to a lawsuit charging desertion, but Cecile's lawyer calmed her down. Peter was still supporting Cecile financially.

The two friends could now see each other freely for a few years until Peter died of a second stroke. Not long after his death Lily married Pierre Picard.

Lavin asked himself if Cecile could have wished Lily dead, even after Peter had died. He talked with a number of her friends and concluded that, while she was vindictive, she was not likely to plan a murder out of revenge after her husband had died.

Chapter 4

Lavin decided that Lily's letters would eventually give him clues to her murder, so he kept digging. He found a series of recent letters with an Indian actress, Vita Banergee, in Bombay. Vita began the letters by telling Lily that an Indian producer, who had helped her in her early career and to whom she felt grateful, insisted on her acting in a series of upcoming B movies, while she held out for films of higher quality. Lily had introduced Vita to producers in France and England with good results. The Indian producer was angry and wrote Lily telling her to mind her own business.

Then, a terrible shock. Vita was murdered by a shot in the back of the head, just a week after Lily's death. The Bombay police had combed through Vita's letters and discovered the correspondence with Lily, and they were quick to connect the two murders. Inspector Fareed Mustafa of the Bombay police called

Death of an Actress

Lavin to discuss possible connections. They agreed that Lavin should go to Bombay to pursue the case. Lavin took Vita's letters with him to show to Mustafa.

The Indian police put him in the elegant Taj Hotel on the water next to the large arch, the English "Gateway to India." Over an elaborate Indian meal on the night of the Frenchman's arrival, the two policemen talked mostly about policing and obligatory "war stories" but also compared the two murders.

Vita had also been killed in her apartment and left lying the same way, face up and arranged as if sleeping. This suggested the same killer. But it seemed a bit far-fetched that whoever shot Vita would think it necessary to also kill Lily over Vita's problems. Revenge for the help that Lily had given Vita made little sense unless Vita's murder had also been a revenge killing.

The two detectives drove out to the Bollywood studios in Bombay to see the producer in question, Vijay Appapurna. He was a rotund, middle-aged man, who received them graciously but warily.

"Gentlemen. I am willing to help you solve these two terrible murders. Two beautiful women killed. I can hardly believe it."

Mustafa went right to the chase. "Vita was unhappy with your pressure on her to act in your films, and you were unhappy with Lily for helping Vita to act elsewhere." It was not a question but a statement of fact.

Appapurna appeared not so much flustered as angry.

"Unhappiness in business is not an excuse for murder. Why would anyone angry at Lily also kill Vita? I made a good deal of money from her movies."

Lavin then asked a question the producer did not expect.

"Did you send anyone to Paris to warn Lily to stay out of your business?"

Appapurna was trapped, and he knew it. Lavin had discovered that one of the Indian producer's men had traveled to Paris from Bombay, not long before Lily's murder. The producer's face was flushed and a dark scowl flashed from his eyes. "What if I did? He went there on business."

"To see Lily and warn her?" Mustafa asked.

"I don't know if he saw her or not. He went to meet with movie distributors. You will have to ask him if he saw Lily."

"Surely you know whether he saw her or not," said Mustafa.

"Well, he did see her briefly about the distribution of one of her movies in India.

"Did he express your unhappiness with what you had done for Vita?" asked Mustafa.

"Yes," said Appapurna, "in passing only."

"What was her response?" asked Mustafa.

"She told him that she would continue to help Vita," said Appapurna, "and it was her business, not ours."

The two detectives said goodbye and went to lunch.

"It doesn't make sense to think that Appapurna would order the murder of both women just out of anger, because they had defied him," said Mustafa.

"I agree," said Lavin. "Will you inquire if he has a history of violence? Absent that, I think that we lack a motive."

They agreed, and a subsequent search of Appapurna's record found nothing. Still, the nearly simultaneous murders could not have been just coincidental. Was there another link between the two women yet to be discovered?

Lavin returned to Paris, promising to keep in touch with Mustafa, and went back to the archive. This time he dug into Lily's business files. It did not take long to find a connection between Lily and Vita They had both acted in a Hungarian production of an English language movie within the past two years. The actors were English speaking, but the producers were Hungarian. The financing of the production was central European, Hungarian, Romanian, and Bulgarian. It was the first production of a new company. The director was Lily's friend Robert Graves, who also acted. The files contained a long correspondence in which lawyers for Graves and the two actors had sued the producers for not paying the actors and director the amounts required by their contracts. The studio had pleaded insufficient funds and called for delay in hopes that the movie would earn more money. The case had been stalled, perhaps deliberately, in the Hungarian courts.

Lavin spoke with Lesage about the case. It had not occurred to Lily's lawyer to mention it earlier in the context of her murder. Lavin and Mustafa then put their staffs to work on the character of the Hungarian moviemakers, particularly to discover the financial sources of the production. The money was primarily from a

Bulgarian source. Further search uncovered a possible link with Bulgarian Mafia funds.

They were still a long way from finding the killer. It would seem to have been the same person, probably a professional. Lavin and Mustafa spoke with the Bulgarian police about possible professional assassins, but no one turned up.

Lavin then had an idea. What if the killer was a woman? Both women had been laid on their sofas as if sleeping. Their beauty was apparent. Would a man, a hired killer, have done this?

They began to search for a woman assassin, but there was very little record, because most hired killers were men. Interpol collected and kept the names of suspects. It was a short list, because once caught, that individual went out of circulation. A few were clever enough not to be caught, at least for a time. Lavin went to Interpol to learn of possible women assassins. He assumed a hired killer because of the nature of the crime; it was so thoroughly professional. There was no record of woman assassins, plenty of murderers but no hired killers.

Chapter 5

These crimes were most puzzling. Two women who knew each other and had acted together had been murdered in the same way at the same time on different continents. Every possible lead had evaporated. The two detectives, in Paris and Bombay, expressed their puzzlement on the telephone for a time and then let the question lie for a time.

Lavin and Sylvanie went to see their daughter Sophie in the country over the weekend, and although Lavin was not supposed to bring his work with him, he raised it at dinner on their patio looking out at the village and Atlantic beyond. Sophie was a psychotherapist, and her husband Bernard was a lawyer who handled criminal defense cases occasionally.

Sophie smoothed back her long, blond hair and asked, "Is it possible that the killers were different people with different motives?"

"Yes, but how explain the identical character of the murders?" her father asked.

"Perhaps the second murder was a deliberate copy-cat killing?" asked Sylvanie.

They all looked puzzled, including Sophie.

"It was just a thought, but I cannot complete it," she said.

After a silence, Anton suggested, "the second killer may have copied the manner of Lily's murder to throw police off, to get them to think that one person in Paris killed them both."

Lavin was thinking.

"The death scene in Lily's apartment was described in the newspapers and on television. I learned that it was widely known in Bombay, the Hollywood of India."

He was grateful for the help his family always gave him and left for Paris on Monday morning with fresh hope but no new leads. Once in his office, he went back through his notes of interviews and Lily's letters. He noticed little that was fresh or new, but Lily's sister, Marguerite, had casually mentioned that an Italian actress had been upset when Lily won a movie part that she, the Italian, had wanted. He did not have the woman's name and called Giles Francois, Lily's manager, to explore the situation.

"She is probably talking about Gina Simone, with whom Lily competed for more than one part. She is older than Lily and is a fine actress, but age may be slowing her career. I know her slightly. She is very temperamental, and I hear that she is unhappy about having to take on older roles."

"Do you know anything else about her?"

"Not really. You must talk with Alesandro d'Amico, a columnist for an Italian magazine on arts and culture. He will tell you more than you need to know."

Lavin wondered how best to approach the Italian writer? He called a friend, Aldo Alfeo, in the central police headquarters in Rome and asked about Gina Simone and her husband, Alfanso Amerigo.

"Oh, you have a tiger by the tail there Jules," said Alfeo. "Simone is volatile and temperamental, both as an actress and as a public personality. She dresses down headwaiters, demands personal attention in shops and markets, and often writes letters to the papers criticizing anyone who she thinks has crossed her. Her husband owns a giant construction company that does work all over the world, and he is a very rough operator. There are many lawsuits against him, charges of corruption in government contracts, and reports of bribery in his business overseas."

"Has he ever engaged in violence to your knowledge?" asked Lavin.

"There are stories. He employs a number of 'tough guys' who enforce his business goals."

"Has he ever done anything to advance or help his wife's career as an actress?"

"He sent his 'toughs' to break up a strike in one of her movie productions. He thinks that she is a great actress and is very vocal about it."

Lavin asked if Allesandro d'Amico would give him an objective report and was assured that d'Amico kept a detached and critical view of the theatrical world. So he called d'Amico and explained his purpose. They met at the newspaper office in downtown Rome.

The critic was a small man with penetrating eyes and a cigarette dangling from his lips as he talked. Lavin told him that he was investigating the death of Lily Martine and asked, without pausing, "Was there bad blood between Lily and Gina Simone?"

"No question about it," said d'Amico. "It went back years after Lily became a star. Lily did not speak Italian, but Gina spoke both French and English and acted in both languages."

"What was the nature of their rivalry?"

"Lily got parts in international productions that Gina wanted. Lily was younger, and Gina was aging. This bothered Gina terribly. She could have taken parts for older women, many of them in starring roles, but she wanted to be the romantic lead in all of her pictures."

"Did Lily and Gina know each other?"

"Yes, but not well. Gina did not want to appear in public with Lily at the Cannes movie festival for example. She would plant stories about Lily's weaknesses as an actress with her favorite Italian critics, but her efforts were not too successful."

"How did Lily deal with the rivalry?"

"She ignored it. After all, she was winning. She was not a petty person, or so I understand."

"What can you tell me about Gina's husband Alfanso Amerigo?"

"A very bad actor."

D'Amico confirmed Aldo Alfeo's assessment of Amerigo. But Lavin could not build a case on bad character alone. He went back to Alfeo and asked him if there had been any other instances in which Amerigo had used force to help his wife's career. After rummaging through his files, Alveo found a case about ten years ago. Amerigo had been charged with hiring men to rough up an actor who his wife wanted out of one of her pictures. The charge had been made but could not be proven in court, and it died.

Lavin began to think that Lily's murder could have been such a case. Was there a sufficient pretext for such action by Amerigo?

He went back to d'Amico and asked, "Was there the possibility of Lily and Gina competing for a recent part that Lily won?"

"I should have told you," said d'Amico. "Lily won a starring role in an Anglo-American production of a remake of Ernest Hemingway's "For Whom the Bell Tolls." I know that Gina wanted the part very much. It would have an international audience, but she wanted to please her Italian fans as well as win that starring role. She was very vocal in her unhappiness and blamed the producers for prejudice against Italian actors."

"Would Gina have gotten the part if Lily had not been available?"

She might have gotten it but one cannot know.

Lavin could surmise connections but still had to uncover them. He went back to Alfeo and asked, "Can you identify the men who did the rough work for Amerigo? I would like to see if they might be connected in any way to Lily's death."

Alfeo gave him five names and put his staff to work to find possible travel arrangements from Rome to Paris at the time of Lily's murder. Two names came up. They were called in by the police for interviews. They were both hard looking men. One had been a boxer and the other an Italian marine. They were interviewed separately by Alfeo. Lavin did not speak Italian, but he observed from the window of a sound booth with a translator.

Both men admitted going to Paris for different reasons. The first went to see a soccer match, and the second said that he had been visiting a cousin. Inquiry showed that the soccer match had been the previous week, and the cousin was not at the given address.

The questioning became more intense. Had someone sent them, and if so, who? Neither man would name Amerigo. One said that he was acting as a secret courier for a private person who did not wish to be named. The other refused to name his purpose.

Then Alfeo decided to play the "Prisoner's Dilemma" game. If both stayed quiet they might escape arrest. But neither could be sure that the other would be quiet. Acting from that concern, it would be rational for one to confess and blame the other one.

The questioning continued for two days and both kept quiet. But one seemed to be weakening. He admitted that they were supposed to call on Lily and try to persuade her to abandon the plum part. They were to be rough if necessary. He said that he had backed out, and his partner had called on her alone. The second man told the same story but said that the other man had shot her when she started to call the police. Neither one had meant to kill her.

Further questioning established that both men had called on Lily, and each accused the other of shooting her. She had been shot from behind, because she was so beautiful that they could not shoot her when her face was turned to them. She had turned to call the police, and one shot did it. It had been a stupid thing to do, because they only talked with her, but one said that they feared their employer if they were arrested and his name was brought into the story.

Both men were charged with murder. Lavin left the question of what the police would do about Amerigo to Alfeo and returned to Paris.

This still left the question of responsibility for Vita's death.

Lavin called Fareed Mustafa in Bombay to tell the Italian story. He offered to help find Vita's killer. The copy-cat hypothesis might be a good place to end up, but where would they start? Mustafa would go to Budapest and talk with the producers of the movie in which Lily and Vita had acted and which was the arena for the existing litigation. Conversations with the movie people yielded little. They insisted that any possible legal or financial reasons for eliminating Vita would not remove the lawsuits by Lily and Vita, because their estates had continued them. Conversations with the Hungarian police yielded nothing, not only because they were defensive about the Western police but also because they could not provide any clues about assassins in Eastern Europe.

Death of an Actress

Mustafa went back to Bombay discouraged. Once home, he looked into Vita's past life and learned that she had recently broken off a long-term affair with a prominent Indian actor. According to several reports, the actor had been furious and had harassed her in person and on the telephone and computer. Vita had become alarmed and had reported the incidents to the police, but the reports had never reached the homicide division.

Mustafa called the actor in and, after considerable grilling, he confessed to killing her. He had read of the details of Lily's murder and had decided to copy the murder exactly in order to complicate the crimes and throw suspicion to Paris rather than Bombay.

Lavin and Mustafa celebrated their victories quietly and resolved to work together again should the occasion arise. Jules Lavin and Sylvanie took a short vacation in Deauville with Sophie, Peter, and two beloved grandchildren. Just as they were packing to return to Paris, the Inspector received a telephone call about a murder in the Louvre.

A MYSTERIOUS MURDER

A Mysterious Murder

Chapter 1

It was a busy April day at the Louvre in Paris. A number of viewers were standing in front of the small portrait of the Mona Lisa, craning their necks and standing on tiptoe to see the painting. Fred Evans, an insurance executive from Kansas City, and his wife Margaret, were among them. They were on the second day of their first trip to Paris. It was very exciting for them. They had seen the Venus de Milo and the Winged Victory statues, and the Mona Lisa was next on their list.

Fred was standing on tiptoe and looking around shoulders when he suddenly fell to the floor. Margaret assumed that he had lost his balance, but he did not get up after attempts to help him. Margaret screamed, the ushers came and carried Fred to a side room and then to an ambulance outside.

The doctor in the Hopital Hotel-Dieu assumed a fatal heart attack, because Fred was not breathing and could not be revived. However his sharp eyes noticed a fresh puncture wound on Fred's left arm.

Margaret was taken back to her hotel with their traveling friends, Jim and Ethel Philips, also from Kansas City. Once the medical people had examined Fred, they concluded that he had been poisoned by a hypodermic needle in his arm. This was murder and the Sureté officials knew whom to assign to the case, Inspector Jules Lavin.

Lavin had been in the country with his wife and his daughter's family when the call came. He arrived home on Sunday afternoon and went to work. He requested an autopsy after viewing the body and then went to the Hotel Regina at 2 Place des Pyramides near the Louvre.

Margaret was still crying when Lavin entered the suite she was sharing with the Philips. She wanted them there as support for her. He knew the difficulty of the conversation to come but was experienced in such situations. He told her the nature of Fred's death, which was even more of a shock than a heart attack. Who on earth would want to kill Fred? It must be a terrible mistake. Neither she nor the Philips knew of any enemies. Fred had been a happy, successful businessman in Kansas City, active in civil affairs, and a respected person.

Lavin immediately thought of mistaken identity but said nothing about it. Margaret was anxious to take Fred home to their children and friends for burial, but Lavin asked her to wait for a day or two for the autopsy, to which she gave permission. The Philips would stay as well.

On Monday morning, Lavin called the bureau of detectives of the Kansas City police and asked for information about Fred Evans. It did not take long for the reply to come that Evans had been a well-regarded citizen who had never been in trouble with the law. He had never sued anyone or been sued. His career in business, while successful, was unremarkable. He was semi-retired.

Lavin encouraged Margaret to return home and made sure that he could contact her easily. She was to let him know if anything suspicious occurred. He then asked himself what to do next. How could he find a man in Paris who looked like Fred Evans?

Sergeant Vincent Richard, who was always at Lavin's right hand, suggested an examination of photos of men who had recently been murdered in Paris to look for resemblance to

Fred Evans. The Inspector thought that this was a good idea and an assignment for the sergeant. It was a thankless task, comparing photographs of men who had died by violence, and it was fruitless. Bonnet suggested that even recent killings would tell nothing. They would have to wait until the real target was killed.

They did not wait long. André Boyer was found dead in an art gallery on the Rue de Rivoli, perhaps on a busman's holiday. He did resemble Fred Evans, a round face, puffy cheeks, a double chin, light brown hair. He had been killed by a hypodermic needle just like Fred.

Boyer had been an art dealer in the business of buying and selling paintings. He had never been convicted of a crime, but the police had picked up rumors from time to time that he might have been engaged in the illegal buying and selling of stolen paintings. He had never been arrested, but the rumors continued. He had traveled a good deal around Europe, including several trips to Russia in recent years.

Lavin knew of the spectacular murder of a Russian émigré in London in recent years and wondered if there could be a parallel crime in Paris. If so, and this was a hunch, perhaps there could be a Russian link. He called his friend at

A Mysterious Murder

Interpol, Maurice Coors, and asked about the theft of art in France and its disposition elsewhere. Coors knew a great deal. "The theft is most often from homes and small private collectons. The paintings then disappear into an invisible market, presumably of wealthy buyers, who keep them. They seldom appear in any markets for resale."

Lavin was intrigued. "So it's just a case of burglary in the first instance?"

"Yes, despite elaborate burglar alarms, even armed guards, the thieves know how to debug alarms, bribe guards, butlers, and maids, learn when families are away for periods of time, and take what they want. They are seldom caught."

"How do you know where the paintings go?"

"Most of the time we don't. They most often go to countries such as Russia, China, Pakistan, and Malaysia, where the police are ineffective, often corrupt, and the art is not available to a wide audience."

"How do you know all this if thieves and buyers are seldom caught?"

"We strike a hit once in a while that confirms the larger pattern. The burglars are caught, either in the acts of theft or in the transport if the art. We can discover where the art is going, but the purchase on the other end is often obscure, and done through middlemen. But we have cracked a few cases and embarrassed, and even arrested and convicted, some buyers. But this is the exception rather than the rule. Honest police in the host countries, if there any, may be knowledgeable about 'fences' who are go-betweens linking sellers and buyers."

Lavin asked Coors if he could give him the names of people who had been caught and convicted of art theft in France in recent years. It was a short list, only a few names. The name of the murdered man was not on it. Coors also gave his friend a list of recent thefts of French art from collections in France, almost all from private homes, that had not been resolved.

The next step for Lavin was to explore the den of thieves. Where to begin? This was a new subject for him, but there was a bureau within the Sureté that dealt with the theft of all "objets d'art." He called Denis Lemaire for help, and they met over lunch in a café in the Place Vendome.

A Mysterious Murder

Lavin set the picture for Lemaire and received the help he needed.

"Your murdered man, Boyer, was a conduit between the sellers and buyers of art across a number of countries," said Lemaire. "We suspected him of dealing in stolen art, because we caught him once. He escaped conviction with the defense that he did not know the art was stolen, but we were pretty sure that he was guilty."

"What might his murder tell us about his illegal activities?" asked Lavin.

"Nothing on the surface, but we can explore the underground of stolen art to try to find out."

It seemed implausible that Boyer was murdered by the potential purchasers of illegal art unless he was trying to cheat them in some way. Such an act would seem too severe, because he presumably controlled the art itself. Such an act might prevent any purchase at all. So Lavin decided to look at Boyer's standing in the world of illegal art in France. He had to go into the art underground again.

He found a former dealer in stolen art who had just been released from prison at the age of seventy, Louis Fabre. Lavin and Richard called on Fabre at his cottage in a small town outside Paris, where he lived with his wife Clarice. Before they began to talk, Fabre announced that he was retired.

"Can you tell us about your career?" Lavin asked.

"I won't to go into particulars," Fabre said with a slight smile. "You might come after me again. I did not steal art or sell it directly to buyers. Rather, I was a conveyer of goods to a buyer from the persons who stole them. My job was to find the connections, and I did this well, working with years of alliances of sellers and buyers all over the world."

He was asked if violence was ever involved in the work and replied that it was rare. Business transactions were amicable for the most part.

Lavin then asked if he knew or had known of Andre Boyer.

"I knew him over many years. We did the same kind of work, except that he ran a legitimate art gallery. He engaged in the traffic of stolen paintings as a lucrative sideline."

"Were there many of you in France?" asked Lavin.

"Perhaps ten at the most," said Fabre. "We usually worked alone, but one group emerged in recent years that has tried to push independent dealers like us out of the trade. They have been trying to create a worldwide market."

"How have they done this?" asked Lavin.

"By underpricing the competition of independents with the intent of raising their prices in the long run," said Fabre. "They have also used strong arm tactics against us, smashing up our homes and warehouses and beating up a few people."

Lavin needed to connect Boyer's murder to the activities of a dealer in France with whom he was perhaps in competition for a client. He decided that he had to talk with someone who had known Boyer and his personal world. Who would this be? Boyer had not been married and had lived alone in a small Paris apartment. His store had closed, and the two employees had disappeared.

Boyer had eaten his meals, for the most part, at a small neighborhood café near his apartment, the Café de la Fleurs. Lavin went round to talk with the owner and proprietor, Armand Roux.

Roux was a short, round man with a deadpan face, who was wary of any policeman. He claimed to know nothing of Boyer other than the fact that he had been an art dealer. Even if Roux knew more, he was not obliged to tell Lavin and might implicate himself if he said anything else.

"Did Boyer have any friends who came to the café with him?" Lavin asked.

"He sometimes came with a woman," said Roux, "but I never knew her name."

"Do you know where she lived?"

"I think in the neighborhood, just as he did."

Lavin found out the name of the gendarme who regularly patrolled the neighborhood and asked if he knew of Boyer and a possible lady friend.

"Yes, I remember him before he was murdered. Her name is Simone David. She lives near Boyer's apartment and was greatly distressed when he was killed."

Lavin rang the bell to her apartment and told the answering female voice who he was and why he wished to see her. She buzzed him in and was waiting on the landing before her door as he walked up to the second floor. She was a short, pretty woman who invited him into her simply but nicely furnished apartment. A few colorful paintings hung on the white walls. She was nervous.

Lavin began in a calm manner. "Were you a long-time friend of M. Boyer?"

"Yes. We had known each other for years. I worked as an appraiser of art work, and he often brought items to me for appraisal before he put them on the market."

"Why do you think he was murdered?"

"I do not know Inspector. I am still shocked by his death. There was nothing about his business that would explain murder."

"Why do you mention his business rather than some other aspect of his life?"

She seemed flustered for a moment. "His life was centered on his gallery. He had no family. We were friends but not lovers, but we did occasionally take trips together to art shows."

"Who inherits the business?"

"I am embarrassed to tell you that I do. But his estate is worth perhaps twenty thousand Euros. He rented the gallery, owned none of the paintings, and left only a small number of securities, which also will go to me."

Lavin asked the next question in hopes of opening a new avenue without mentioning fraud. "Did he sell many paintings to purchasers abroad?"

Simone did not falter at the question. "There were some Russian clients. I think they were newly rich oligarchs with lots of money who wanted to show off their new wealth with newly acquired art."

Lavin took a leap. "Could any of these sales been for stolen paintings?"

"André would never have taken part in that kind of thing. It would have brought more money than he had ever had."

Lavin decided that Simone was telling the truth insofar as she knew it. He thanked her and left in search of a riddle about Boyer's reputation.

Chapter 2

The killing of Boyer suggested to Lavin that the murdered man was perhaps standing in the way of someone who wanted to take his place in a transaction. Louis Fabre had suggested the possibility. Lavin returned to Denis Lemaire to ask about new kinds of buyers and sellers.

"Fabre had it right," Lemaire told him. "Our problem is that such groups are new, and we only know about them through reputation on the grapevine. One might do better by tracing them from the buyer end, for example, in Russia or wherever."

"How would we go about that?"

"Go to Russia and try to find a report of French paintings that have gone to private buyers."

"But if such sales are legal what is there to discover?"

"Not all sales are legal, and the Russian police will overlook stolen art if it goes to people well connected to the Putin regime."

"How can I rely on the police then?"

"There is one private art firm in Moscow that appears to be honest. We have worked with them a few times. They may able to help you, but secretly and quietly. I will give you a list of paintings stolen from French homes and small museums in the past few months. You can see if they know about any possible leads where some of this art may have gone. The director of the group is named Arkady Litvinoff. I will send him a message that you will call him. You may even want to go to Russia."

This was an intriguing idea for Jules. But he had first to study the list of stolen French paintings carefully. Lemaire sent them along to him. The most appealing of the group were three paintings by Matisse stolen from a home in Cannes. They were gorgeous watercolors of Mediterranean scenes along the coast of North Africa. These would surely be enjoyed in a Russian winter.

Lavin understood that Litvinoff spoke French. Everyone in policing now spoke English, so Lavin was gratified to speak his own language. He called the agency and arranged a time for a conversation.

Their talk was inconclusive. Lavin explained that he hoped to track French art thieves from possible Russian buyers but had to admit that he had no knowledge of such buyers. He simply had a list of stolen French paintings. He had sent the list to Latvinoff by fax.

"I cannot tell you immediately," the Russian said, "but let me snoop around a bit. We hear about stolen art in circles that we may not explore. I will see what I can find out. Some of our informants have been in homes with stolen art, seldom as guests but often as servants or delivery or repair people. I will take soundings."

Lavin heard nothing for a month. In the meantime, he went underground in the criminal world to see what he could learn about the world of art thievery. He learned that the business had gone corporate with firms replacing individuals in stealing, transporting, and selling art. It had become an international business with rich clients in many nations. Informants identified a few names and locations, but he was not after art thieves as such. He was in search of a killer.

Chapter 3

Litvinoff finally came back with some information. The three Matisse paintings were in the home of a Moscow oligarch. Lavin was uncertain what to do next. He had no authority in Russia to investigate crimes. He could notify the Moscow police and ask for help, but Litvinoff cautioned that he might not get it.

Lavin finally hit on an idea. He wrote the oligarch, Ivan Gorky, telling him he understood that he had the Matisse paintings and that they had been stolen in France. He did not suggest that Gorky might have known that the paintings were stolen but asked how and where Gorky had bought them. There was no reply for some days, and when a letter came, it was from a Russian attorney, Igor Rybakov, speaking for Gorky. The letter said that Gorky had bought the paintings from a reputable art broker in Geneva, who was named. As far as his client was concerned, the sale was legal and valid, and that was the end of the matter.

Lavin discovered soon enough that the supposed art broker in Geneva was no longer in business. He knew that the paintings had been stolen, and he could prove it, so he needed the help of the Russian police. He called Roland Collet of the Quai d'Orsay, the French Foreign Office, who worked in international crime, and explained the situation.

Collet knew of Gorky. He was a rich man but was not particularly close to Putin or the government. He had made his money in real estate and shared it generously with public officials in bribes in regard to properties. He had not had any political ambitions, nor had he ever been active in politics. He was a friend to all and a threat to no one. Collet suggested that one approach might be to find a way to publicize the theft of the paintings so that Gorky would be publicly embarrassed. Perhaps this would make the Russian police cooperative.

There were two ways to do this, and they could be combined. Ask an honest Russian politician to raise the issue of stolen art in the Parliament. This could be done on the basis of a story in one of the few independent newspapers.

It would be a news story reporting that the French had contacted Ivan Gorky about the missing paintings, and that the Swiss broker could not be found. Collet said that he would try to get permission from his superiors for this to happen. It was done, and the French embassy in Moscow would carry out the details.

Again, nothing happened for a good many days, and then Collet sent Lavin two Moscow news stories: the newspaper report and then an account of a parliamentary question about stolen art in Russia. Gorky was named in the first story but not the second.

Chapter 4

Not long after that Lavin received a letter from Gorky's attorney, Igor Rybakov in Moscow, referring him to a Paris lawyer, Armand Dubois. Dubois called and asked if he might call on Lavin. They arranged a date, and at ten in the morning, Armand Dubois, a criminal lawyer whom Lavin knew only by reputation, appeared at his office in the Sureté.

Dubois looked to the policeman to be a very smooth character, a settler of problems and conflicts. He was conservatively dressed with a flower in his buttonhole and sharply creased trousers. His shoes were formal and brightly shined.

Lavin quietly asked Dubois his business.

"I am acting for my Moscow colleague, M. Igor Rybakov, who in turn is acting for M. Ivan Gorky. It concerns the matter of three paintings that M. Gorky bought on the market through a Swiss art broker. It is our understanding that that particular broker is no longer in business. M. Gorky will offer to try to find the broker if it is understood that M. Gorky will not be accused of any crime by the French police. He bought the paintings in good faith."

Lavin was not interested in charging Gorky. That was a matter for the Russian police. He replied by stating his interest, thanking Dubois for his cooperation.

The matter rested there for about two weeks. Then Dubois called on him again.

"M. Gorky has engaged private detectives who have found those who sold him the paintings. They have not been cooperative and have threatened to implicate M. Gorky in art theft if their names are disclosed publicly or even to the Swiss police."

This was frustrating to Lavin to have thieves in the shadows who would not cooperate. He could see that they might fear that naming French collaborators might provoke accusations from their former connections against them. Gorky was still obligated to tell Lavin the names of his suppliers.

Lavin spoke to Dubois the next day. "We must know the names of the Swiss art brokers. We do not expect M. Gorky to discover the

French connection. We will do that, working with Swiss authorities, and leave Gorky out of it altogether."

Dubois listened, consulted, and reported that they would provide one name and address in Geneva but that Gorky would maintain that he had understood that one person to be a legitimate art broker. After a few days, Lavin was given the name of Carlu Crescenco and a street address in Geneva.

A quick check with the Geneva police and Interpol revealed that Crescenco had left the address months ago. His whereabouts were unknown. His name was Corsican. Lavin called a detective friend in Marseilles, Francois Benoit, and asked whom he might best call in Ajaccio, Corsica to ask about Crescenco.

Benoit offered to make the call, because he knew a number of detectives in Ajaccio. He called back in a few minutes.

"They know Crescenco well. He is a first-class rogue who has been in all kinds of crime. He has had a home retreat in the mountains on the southern island. If he is there, they will find him and arrest him for you."

Lavin called the Corsican police, told them of the case, and asked them to find

Crescenco. He told them that, so far as he knew, Crescenco did not know that the police in Geneva were after him. He could, therefore, be taking his ease in his mountain retreat.

The authorities went to Crescenco's house and did not find him but made inquiries in Ajaccio and found him living with a girlfriend in a beach house. He was arrested and held for questioning.

Lavin flew to Ajaccio. He had to confront the man face to face in order to find out the names of French accomplices who had actually stolen the paintings and perhaps killed two men.

Crescenco was not at all happy to be in jail. He was a smooth looking character dressed in a flashy suit and bright yellow shoes.

"You have no cause to detain me, Inspector," he said in broken French. "What is the charge?"

Crescenco's lawyer, who looked equally smooth, also asked for the charge.

Lavin explained the identification of Crescenco by Ivan Gorky.

This was immediately denied.

Lavin then reported that Gorky's lieutenants were willing to identify Crescenco as the man who delivered the painting to them. He knew that this was not the case but said it anyway in hopes of frightening Crescenco. It worked.

"I am not an art thief," said Crescenco. "I am only the conduit between the sellers and the buyers."

"Well then," Lavin told him, "You will be able to tell us the names of the sellers, the actual people who stole the painting."

Crescenco clearly did not want to do this. Lavin supposed that the Frenchmen were business associates with whom he might work in the future.

"I do not want to charge you with the theft of the paintings," he told Crescenco. "But I will do so if you do not cooperate. We will find them and charge you along with them."

Crescenco was a rogue but not a fool. "I will give you a name," he said. "But I want my identity to be secret."

Lavin promised that the person named would not be told the source of his identification.

Crescenco then said, "I suggest that you look for Antoine Perret in Marseilles."

Lavin went back to Francois Benoit in Marseilles and was told that Perret was in jail serving a sentence for art theft. It was a short sentence for stealing a statue from a small museum.

Benoit and Lavin went to see Perret and told him that they were investigating the theft of the three Matisse paintings and their sale to a Russian. Perret professed ignorance. Their only evidence was the word of Carlu Crescenco. It was pretty thin.

Benoit and Lavin went back to police headquarters and then out to lunch to a small café. Then Lavin had an idea. As he was dipping his mussels in a dish of hot butter, he asked Benoit, "Why don't we talk to the usual suspects among art thieves and see if we can work back to Perret?"

They began to go down a list of names of men and women who had been arrested for art theft, a fairly small group, and found an association between Stella de France, a known criminal, and several men who seemed to have worked with her.

The group was brought into the Marseilles police station. There were four of them. Ms. de France was clearly the most intelligent and appeared to be de facto leader. She was about forty, slender, and good looking in a hard sort of way.

She denied any role in stealing the Matisse paintings, so Lavin hit her hard. "Whoever stole the Matisse paintings also killed two men. Can you help us there?"

She had not expected the question and seemed a little rattled.

Lavin followed up. "The theft of art is one thing. Murder is another. If we could learn more about the murder, we could be more lenient about robbery."

This was a gamble, because the evidence about the theft itself was so limited. He hoped that de France would think that he knew more than he actually knew.

Stella asked to see her lawyer, who was, in fact, also representing the other three men brought in with her.

Lavin and Benoit waited two days and then brought Stella back for an interview, with her lawyer, a Marseilles avocat in criminal law named Hubert da Silva, who spoke first. "My clients will provide information if the charges could be reduced to misdemeanors."

This was what Lavin had been looking for. He had tricked the thieves. With a complete absence of honor, they all made statements that Perret had been their leader and that he had ordered the murder of the two small time art dealers in order to clear the way for his own group in the market for stolen art. This by itself was no honor among thieves, but subsequent inquiry tied Perret to a syndicate for art theft on a larger scale. Subsequent arrests by police in several European cities uncovered an organization that was seeking to corner the market for the theft of art. This was enough to convict Perret for second degree murder and a prison sentence exceeding that for theft.

Lavin had been feeling his way from one suspect to the next. But the structure of the crime had always been clear in his mind. He simply had to fill in the unknowns. This was his way of deducing crimes from an initial construct that, once in place, had served him well.

WITHOUT A GUN

Chapter 1

Inspector Jules Lavin had not carried a gun since his days as a young patrolman. He kept up his supposed skills with a pistol on the practice firing range, but that was not quite the same thing in self-protection in close quarters. He was a specialist in murder, and it was as such that he was unwittingly drawn into the pursuit of terrorists.

It all began from Paris in Amman, the capitol of the small country of Jordan. A French woman, who gave her name as Arlette, had followed her lover to Syria, where he had joined ISIS. He was also French, of Algerian descent. She did not give his name. He was not a soldier but a computer operator. After six months, they had decided to defect and had gotten to Jordan secretly, where they were staying with a protector. She wrote that she would be at St. Xavier church every afternoon at five and would be wearing a bandana of a different color each day, sometimes red, blue, or yellow.

The Consul decided to send a man to meet Arlette, and just before five the next day, he entered the gloomy church. Finally he saw the red bandana and took the pew behind her. The church was almost empty, and neither pew was filled. He coughed, and as she looked around, he smiled. She rose to light a votive candle, and as she sat down, he crossed himself.

"Arlette?" he asked.

"Yes,"

"What shall we do?"

"We will be on the terrace of the café across from the church at ten tonight. Can you pick us up?"

"Yes, white car."

That was settled. The man went back to work and made the arrangements. The white car arrived at ten, but the couple were not at the café. As the Consel's men looked around, they saw two inert bodies at the door of the church. It was Arlette and her friend; each had been shot several times.

The crime was murder, but Jules Lavin did not expect to be called. He had not worked with terrorists. But he was called.

His Commissionaire told him, "Jules, Arlette told us in her note that she had begun her journey to Syria in Stuttgart, Germany. ISIS agents met her there and put her on a train to Istanbul, and agents there met her and sent her to Syria."

"Do we know how she met these people?" asked Lavin.

"No. They could not let her escape with such knowledge."

"What do you want me to do?"

"Simple. Find out how ISIS is getting their people in and out of France."

"That is a big order. I know about murder, not transportation."

"Nonsense, these ISIS thugs are murderers. I want you to catch them all." This was said with a slight but grim smile.

Lavin went home to pack his bag.

Sylvine was not at all happy about the assignment. "You come home every night for dinner," she said. "The murderers you catch do not harm you. I do not want you involved with terrorists. It is too dangerous."

"This is just one brief assignment to make inquiries," said Lavin. "I will only be away overnight. Have a nice dinner for me when I return."

Lavin sounded brave, but he was somewhat worried to be pursuing terrorists. He was holding a tiger by the tail. He kissed Sylvine good-bye, took a taxi to the Gare Montparnasse, and boarded a train for Germany.

He was in Stuttgart by five in the afternoon. The Banhoff, train station, was large with high ceilings and a large open concourse. He took a cab to a small hotel and, once he had settled in, went out to dinner, a place called Di Gasthaus Tube, where he ate a small steak and red cabbage and drank a stein of beer, something he never did in Paris.

The next morning, He took a letter from his Commissionaire to the Director of Police and introduced himself. His German was passable since he had served in the army in Germany as a young draftee. He presented his letter and was sent into the office of Herr Waldo Schulze, an imposing man with the face of a warrior.

Schulze read the letter and after a moment, said, "I would love to catch terrorists moving their people through Stuttgart, but we have no evidence of that. Why would Stuttgart be used? We keep track of refugees from Syria, Jordan, and other places as best we can. Most are put in refugee camps and then vetted before they are turned loose. What would you have me do?"

Lavin had no answer and was embarrassed by his muteness. Then he had an idea. "What about moving vans? That would be an efficient, secretive way to move individuals. They could be hidden in trucks apart from the regular loads of the vans."

Herr Schulze was astonished, but he recognized a bright idea. He went to the city directory and found ten moving firms in the city and several more in the metropolitan region of many small cities.

"Now what do we do?" asked Herr Schulze. "We could inquire about the histories and owners of the firms, and their regular routes. The use of such a strategy suggests multiple destinations across western Europe."

This made sense to Lavin, but it was work for the Stuttgart police. He would go home and await their report. His assignment would be at the receiving end should anyone get through.

So he went home, pleased that he had completed his assignment. Now for a nice, juicy murder in Paris.

There was no news from Stuttgart for three weeks. Lavin put it aside in his mind.

Then a call came from Herr Schulze. "We have identified three moving companies as possibilities. Our superiors inform us that we may not move forward without official French cooperation. This is a matter for the European Union."

Lavin was skeptical. Perhaps the high German command wanted to blame the French police for any mishap.

The Commissionaire told Lavin that he should go back, regardless of German hesitation. So off he went, the same bag packed with only a few things, the same hotel, and the same meal in the same restaurant, only this time he had weinerschnitzel.

Chapter 2

Schulze's staff had identified three companies as possible culprits. The first was an Austrian company with an office in Stuttgart. The second was a German firm that had cooperated with the government in Berlin in relocating Syrian refugees. The third was a firm owned by a company in Turkey with an office in Stuttgart, which moved Arab families within Germany. Turkish immigrant workers were part of the German economy.

Lavin sat down with Schulze and his colleagues to discuss what they might best do. The meeting did not last long before they all went out to a Gasthaus for lunch. Lavin didn't want any more weinerschnitzel. Two of the men ordered raw, very fine quality beef, with fried eggs on top. Lavin decided to have an omelet and a small glass of white wine.

The business at hand was how best to watch the three firms without being caught doing so. The owners of the companies appeared to be legitimate, long standing, and without criminal records. The three firms were in sound financial condition. They were family firms in each case.

Lavin and Schulze decided to post hidden police observers at each loading dock. It might be possible to detect people being smuggled onto the moving vans.

Nothing was detected after a week of observation, and Lavin grew tired of weinerschnitzel. Most of the vans were loaded and set off during the day, but on one rainy evening, police saw three men get into a van that was to be filled with furniture and sent to an address in Lyon, France. It had been decided not to intervene at that point but to wait until the van had crossed into France to act. Lavin and two German policemen followed the van and alerted German and French police along the route.

Once the van had crossed into France, Lavin decided to act. The police car stopped the van and found three men inside, secured in a compartment in the back, apart from the furniture. They were clearly Arabs. Lavin called for a police van to take them away, but in the next moment a car drew up, and armed, masked men got out and ordered Lavin and his companions to surrender.

Lavin and his companions were handcuffed to the doors of their car. Their guns and cell phones were taken. Then the released men and their driver were put in the other car and driven away. They were gone by the time Lavin's backup arrived.

He asked himself why he and his companions had not been shot. Terrorists have no scruples. Perhaps, he mused, a big event requiring several men was planned and the terrorists did not want to unnecessarily alarm the French police. It might be that other men were being brought in at various points. He decided to return to Stuttgart to examine the moving company.

The German police arrested the firm's workers from the previous night. They admitted that they had hidden the three men in the van but claimed they were acting under orders. The directions were from the management but without any names attached. Schulze believed them. They were casual workers who were not regular employees. Still, he would hold them for a day or two for investigation.

The firm was owned by a German family. Herr Schulze and Lavin called on Ernest Romer, the owner.

Romer was a man in his late seventies, who had inherited the firm from his father. He denied any knowledge of smuggling. His children were married daughters, who were not involved the management of the company. One nephew, Wily Schroeder, oversaw the direction of day to day operations.

Lavin and Schulze found Schroeder at the firm's offices. He was a bachelor with slightly effeminate manners, who spoke to them with some nervousness.

Schulze bore down hard on him from the outset. "Tell us what you know about smuggling men from Stuttgart into France."

"Why should I know anything?" asked Schroeder.

"Because your name and signature are on the moving order," said Schulze, "and you were at the depot last night before the van left."

Schroeder began to shake with nervousness. "I was trying to help a friend who wanted his three brothers to join him in France."

"But the three men we captured are not brothers," said Schulze. "Who is your friend in France?"

At this point Schroeder sat down and buried his head in his hands but said nothing.

"Were you under any pressure to do this thing?" Lavin asked.

Schroeder raised his eyes. They were filled with tears. "My uncle is a very strict Catholic. He does not approve of gay people. They threatened to tell him about me unless I cooperated."

"Do you know who these people are?" Schulze asked.

"No. They are not Arab. My guess is that they are German criminals who have penetrated the moving business. I do not know their names or addresses. They came to see me in the office."

Herr Schulze was going to arrest Schroeder. He would have liked to have used him to draw in other criminals, but Schroeder was now known to have failed. The criminals would not try him again. So off Schroeder went to jail, and Lavin went home.

The next day, Lavin called a friend at the International Police Organization to ask what was known about criminal smugglers working with terrorists. His friend knew of one case and gave him the name of a Frenchman who was in jail in Strausbourg for smuggling terrorists.

Lavin went to Strausbourg to see Claude Herve. He was in a medium security prison, serving a twenty-year sentence. Herve was a professional criminal who had been involved in burglary, hijacking, and smuggling drugs. Transporting people was a new vocation for him. Lavin took the high road at first. "Are you proud of smuggling Syrian terrorists who would have killed French people had they not been caught?"

"I did not know who they were," said Herve.

"I don't believe you. You saw them, didn't you? Did they look like Frenchmen?"

"No, but I am a soldier in the ranks, not a leader. I just follow orders."

"Does this mean that you have nothing to tell me?"

"I might, but what good would it do me?"

"Are you asking for a relief from your sentence? How do I know that you know anything?"

"I might know the main smugglers and help you find them. But I would need a reward."

Lavin said nothing more but indicated that he might be back.

He returned to Paris and raised the question with the Commissionaire, Louis Fiquet, who was reluctant to give Herve a reduced sentence. Why put a committed criminal back on the street, even after a lapse of time?

Lavin agreed. "Let me see what else I can find about Herve. Perhaps he has friends among criminals who are more patriotic and might help us."

Chapter 3

Lavin looked back into Herve's criminal record and found the names of previous associates, some of whom were in jail. One man, Georges Fulbert, had worked with Herve in smuggling stolen art. But they had stopped their collaboration before Herve was arrested. Fulbert was living in a lower middle class suburb of Paris, and rather than call him, Lavin went to see him. Fulbert was not at home, but his concierge said that he was in a nearby café, The Red Cock.

It was late morning, and people were just arriving for lunch. Lavin saw his man, who looked like his police mug shot, perhaps even uglier. He asked the bartender if he would call Fulbert over.

Fulbert was a short, pudgy man, who approached Lavin warily. He knew a policeman when he saw one.

Lavin introduced himself and said that Fulbert was not in trouble. Might they sit down?

"I suppose that you want information," Fulbert said.

"You may be able to help me. I am investigating the smuggling of terrorists into France."

Fulbert frowned. "I will have nothing to do with that. I am a patriot."

"Do you know any human smugglers?"

"I was once approached by a man who talked of this but I refused."

"Was he Claude Herve?"

Fulbert sat up straight and stared at Lavin. "How could you know that?"

"I just know it. Who was Herve working for?"

Fulbert answered that he did not know.

Lavin then told him that a ring of criminals was smuggling large numbers of terrorists into France and that a very bloody attack was being planned. He exaggerated for effect.

"I do know that there is a criminal gang who may be smuggling people," said Fulbert. "They are led by a man named 'Scar' Sicard. Herve was friendly with 'Scar' in the past. That is all I know."

Lavin bought Fulbert a glass of wine, thanked him, and left.

He went back to the Sureté and, with the Commissionaire's permission, he put out an order to all points to find Sicard and bring him in.

Two days went by, and nothing happened. No one could find Sicard.

On the morning of the third day, Lavin was walking along a narrow street in the Marais on his way to lunch when a black car pulled up beside him. Two masked men got out and, at gunpoint, pushed him into the car. They put tape over his mouth, a blindfold over his eyes, and tape around his wrists. No one spoke. They drove in and out of streets for some minutes.

Once they stopped, they roughly pushed Lavin into a building and up three flights of stairs. They put him in a room by himself and locked the door.

He sat on a chair in some discomfort and managed to rip off the blindfold and the tape on his mouth. He was working on his wrist bands when a masked man entered with a tray of bread and cheese. The man put down the tray and said nothing but waited as if he expected the detective to talk.

When Lavin said nothing, the man asked, "Why do you want to chase after terrorists?"

It was not a question Lavin expected.

"Because they want to kill French people. Do you approve of that?"

The man stared at him and then turned and left.

It went on this way for two days. Lavin slept on a narrow bed, used a toilet and sink, and ate sparse meals. Then one day, no one came in.

He tried the door to the room. It was not locked. The apartment was empty. He walked downstairs and called the Sureté from a corner café. In a few minutes, he was back in his office with Sylvine and the Commissionaire. They brought him a crepe and a glass of wine.

"Please explain what has happened," Lavin asked.

The Commissionaire answered,

"Yesterday a group of terrorists entered a schoolyard and shot a number of children and teachers before they were killed themselves by our people. It was a terrible scene, because we had trouble picking out the killers among the others."

"But why did my captors let me go?" asked Lavin.

"They are criminals helping terrorists, but they are Frenchmen. The bloodshed, especially of children, may have been too much for them."

"Why didn't they kill me?" asked Lavin.

"They did not want to be guilty of murder," said the Commissionaire.

"Then, why did they kidnap me in the first place?"

"They may have had orders to do so," said the Commissionaire. "'Scar' Sicard is a killer. But his men thought otherwise. You are very lucky. You deserve some time off."

Sylvine drove him home. They packed light bags and drove off to see their daughter Sophie in the village of Les Veules en Rose on the Normandy coast. They had a lovely week with their grandchildren and lots of good food, sleep, long walks by the sea, and comfortable talks by the kitchen fire in the evening.

Back at work Lavin learned that the terrorist killers at the school had been the same three men that he had arrested from Stuttgart. This sickened him. He had had enough of terrorists. He was a specialist in murder, and he never needed or used a gun.

MURDER IN THE OPERA

Chapter 1

Inspector Jules Lavin was intelligent but not broadly cultured. French universities did not teach criminology, and he wanted to be a policeman, so he studied sociology at the University of Auvergne. He and his wife Sylvine would go to the theater at times, but although she liked opera, he was not keen on it.

He was very good at reading people. When interviewing witnesses or suspects, he never said too much and waited for them to talk, and would pause. They would sometimes rush on to say more than they intended. He could find similarities between characters in plays and people in his work. But the characters in operas were exaggerated beyond proportion, and besides, they wore silly costumes, unlike real people. Lavin was the ultimate realist. He felt somehow out of place when the

Commissionaire of Police sent him to investigate the murder of a tenor of the opera.

The small opera company, The Theater of the Arts, was enjoying a working retreat at a hotel in the Loire Valley when Alain Bergeron, a most promising young tenor, was found dead in his room. It was last day of the gathering, and they were to leave that morning.

Lavin was enjoying a cup of latte with Sylvine at home when the telephone rang, and the Commissionaire suggested nicely in haste that Lavin must go to the Loire Valley. So off he went, telling Sylvine that he might not be back that night.

It took him an hour to reach the small inn that had been rented for the weekend by the Opera company. The local police had taken charge so that all members of the company had been identified and told to stay put. The medical report was clear. Bergeron had been stabbed in the back of his head in a way to create instant death with minimal bleeding. One strong hold around the neck of a sleeping man and one stroke with the knife would do the job.

Lavin's first question was whether the inn's doors were locked at night, and the answer was yes. Nor was there any sign of forced entry through doors or windows. This suggested to Lavin that the killer might be in the company.

The artistic director was Charles de France, a tall, angular man with flourishing white hair and deep set blue eyes. He spoke in musical tones, suggesting to Lavin that he might have once been a singer.

"This is a terrible thing, Inspector," said de France. "Alain was on his way to a fine operatic career, surely beyond this company. But he was our star tenor, and we needed him badly for the season, which begins in a month."

"What can you tell me about him?" asked Lavin.

"He was thirty years old, single, and devoted to his craft. I cannot tell you about his private life, because I try to avoid knowledge of the lives of my singers. Such knowledge would exhaust me and surely complicate my work."

Lavin took this with a grain of salt but admired de France's sagacity. He would have to explore such things himself. He told de France that he would interview members of the company in turn in the parlor of the inn. They would then be free to leave. He asked for all home addresses as well.

According to M. de France the twenty members of the company were a mix of aspiring newcomers on their way up and established performers on their way down. The veterans taught the aspirants, although not without some jealously. No one wanted to be a fading star. But the leading roles were filled by the experienced singers, and the company had a high professional and popular reputation and filled the seats in its relatively small theater in Paris. They often did new or avant garde operas, which tested the path for the larger companies.

De France assembled the entire company in the inn's parlor. It was small, and some had to stand.

The inspector spoke quietly and firmly.

"I regret holding you here, but this tragedy must be investigated. I hope that you can all go home tomorrow, but, of course, I may want to talk with you individually once we are back in Paris."

He said that he would talk with them according to their vocal attainments, sopranos, contraltos, tenors, baritones, and basses, of whom he was told, there was one. A chesty man put his hand up in acknowledgement. Ten singers were the chorus, and they filled the roles of the principals when necessary.

There were two sopranos, Adelaide Armand, a well-regarded and experienced star and Charlotte Levy, a young, highly touted singer. They did not seem comfortable with each other. Armand was just short of glamorous with long auburn hair and bright green eyes. Levy was small and dark with a pretty pointed face and a nice smile. Lavin asked them if they alternated the same roles, and they said no, they usually sang different parts. Still, they were on stage together often and could be compared by audiences and critics. The older woman seemed dismissive of the younger.

Lavin asked M. Armand what she knew about the dead man.

She hesitated and said that she knew very little. He had been charming and talented but had kept to himself and was intent on his career.

M. Levy expressed a certain surprise at this report but said nothing. She had not known Bergeron well. They had each been in the company for only one season.

The inspector told Levy that she might go but asked M. Armand to stay a minute. He paused to see a nervous look on M. Armand's face. "Perhaps you know more about our tenor than you said?" he asked.

There was a long silence and then she said,

"You are very discerning, Inspector. Alain and I were lovers for the past year, but he threw me over, whether for someone else I don't know."

"You were upset?"

"Of course. But I meant him no harm. I have had lovers in the past and hope to have them in the future."

"Do you know of anyone who might wish to harm M. Bergeron?"

"No. He was a good young man who cared only for his career, which was promising."

Lavin thanked her and called for the other tenor. He was Adam Basset, a stocky man with wavy black hair and a diffident air, as if he would rather not be there.

"What can you tell me about M. Bergeron?" asked Lavin.

"He was new in the company, and I am the established tenor," said Basset. "I was jealous at first, because he had some talent, but I am the far better singer so I relaxed."

M. de France says that he had a good future ahead of him."

"Perhaps so, but perhaps not."

"I gather that you were not friends."

"He kept to himself."

The two baritones and the bass seemed to know very little about the dead man.

The contralto, Carole Janvier, was very chatty. "Adelaide was smitten with Alain," she said, "and when he broke it off, she threw a pitcher of water at him in her apartment, breaking a lamp. I know, because he told me. Adam was jealous of him. Alain was very talented and had real promise. These ensemble groups are rife with rivalries."

Carole was an experienced vocalist in her mid-career but did not seem to worry about her future. "My husband is a stockbroker," she said, "and while I love to sing, I have another life, which many of us do not. Some of us are vagabonds."

She was amusing, but Lavin pressed on.

"M. de France, the director, tells me that he does not want to know about the private lives of his singers. Is that true?"

"Nonsense. He scoops up the gossip and knows us all like a book. It helps him direct in that he knows our moods and manages us accordingly."

"Can you give me an example?"

"Well, when Adelaide was upset about Alain, he knew how to talk with her about her role as Manon in a way to settle her down."

"Counseling was within his directing technique?"

"Yes. He is a prima donna himself, having been a fine baritone, but he understands singers and how the drama of opera plays into their personalities."

This was a very enjoyable woman, but Lavin had to move on.

He next talked to Yves Simon, the director of the chorus. "Did you know M. Bergeron well?" he asked.

"No," said Simon. "He was only with us last season. But I observed him and knew that he had great talent."

"How would you compare his talent to that of M. Basset, the other tenor?"

"Adam is very good. He can hold the stage with most tenors, but Alain was special, even unusually good."

"Do any of the singers in the chorus know Adam well?"

Roland Dumas is an aspiring tenor, and he did not know him well, but I think that he would have liked a starring role in the company."

"Was he jealous of Alain?"

"I don't think so. He just wanted to get ahead. He would have done so in time. He is very good."

Lavin had finished his interviews and told de France that they might return to Paris.

Chapter 2

Lavin got home later that evening, and Sylvine had a good lamb chop and glass of red wine waiting for him. She watched him eat and saw that he was mulling over the uncertainties in his mind. After dinner, he sat in his comfortable chair and talked out loud while she listened.

"The lead soprano was angry at Bergeron, and she could probably strike in a crime of passion. But somehow, I do not think so. The two tenors were jealous of Alain, but would they have killed him just to advance in the company? It seems unlikely. I must look further and find better clues."

"Where will you find them?" asked Sylvine.

"I know a music critic who helped me with a case once. I think I'll call him."

The next day, he called the critic, Guy Dione, who wrote for Le Figaro, and arranged to have lunch with him. They met in a small café near the paper. He had told Dione about the case and had learned that Dione knew the company well.

Lavin began, "I gather that this is a fine collection of singers?"

"Yes indeed," said Dione. "They put on intimate productions portraying only the leading roles with a small chorus, but they are widely admired."

"Is Adelaide Armand on the way down in her career?"

"No, she has years yet to sing, but the leading soprano roles will go to younger women in time."

"What do you know of her personal life?"

"She is a beautiful woman who has had many lovers. I think she would like to be married, but an operatic career is not conducive to a stable marriage." Dione then volunteered the report, "She was heard to say in a theater restaurant recently of Bergeron, 'I'll kill him,' but I can't imagine that she meant it."

"What was the difference in their ages?"

"He was thirty, and she is near forty if not quite there yet. That difference in age is nothing among artists."

Lavin silently agreed and pressed on. "Bergeron seems to have had little private life. Is that the case?"

"Yes, at present, aside from Adelaide. He was married as a younger man but very briefly. They had a child. I think that Alain was more interested in opera and his career than in family. He simply left them. His wife got a divorce eventually."

It was past time to talk with Isabelle Piquet, Bergeron's former wife. She was in the Paris telephone book, and Lavin called her. He explained his intent, and she agreed to see him.

Isabelle lived in a small apartment in the St. Germain area. Lavin rang the bell, and the door was opened to reveal an exceptionally pretty young woman. Isabelle Piquet had taken back her maiden name. She was blonde with blue eyes and had a lithe figure. Lavin thought that he would never leave such a woman for an operatic career.

Her apartment was richly furnished, and she was handsomely dressed. Lavin asked her, out of curiosity, if she had a profession.

"Yes indeed. I teach literature at the Sorbonne."

"What were you doing when your husband left?"

"I was working on my graduate degree. It was difficult financially, especially having a small son, but my father helped me, and now I am established in a good career."

"I am sorry to bring you into this story, but you may be able to help me understand Alain Bergeron. What can you tell me about him, and what you know of his life after your marriage?"

"He was a real charmer. I loved him. And yet, he was consumed by ambition to be a great opera singer. He was off singing in different productions immediately after we were married, and it became clear that a regular married life was not possible for him."

"Did you accept this?"

"After a time, I did. We had a baby, but he saw very little of either of us in our two years of marriage. I loved him still but I had to let him go."

"What have you seen of him in later years?"

"He kept in touch, letting me know about his career. Occasionally he would visit little Jacques, but he never really got to know him. I also learned about him from my brother, Andre, who directs a small opera company in Aix."

"Was Alain self-centered?"

"Yes, very much so. He was so good looking and charming that I was swept off my feet, but I saw, in time, that he cared primarily about himself and his career."

Lavin had learned the name of another person to whom to talk, Andre Piquet. He took the train down to Aix in Provence and met Andre in the office of his small opera company. Lavin told him of his inquiries to date and asked Piquet for anything that he might know about Bergeron and his life that might be helpful to him.

"I knew him primarily as my brother in law. I never liked him much, because I think he took advantage of my sister in more ways than one. He deserted her and also borrowed money from her, which he never paid back."

"Did you have any professional relationship with him?"

"Only one. I was an assistant director of a company in which Alain was singing. He could not get along with the director, and eventually insisted to the manager that the director be replaced in the production. He virtually threatened to quit otherwise. He prevailed. The director stepped aside."

"How could a novice tenor have such influence?"

"The small company needed him, and he was very talented even then."

Lavin took a walk around Aix before he caught the train. The old buildings, fountains, and churches were charming. He had grown up in a rather drab town in the Auvergne.

Chapter 3

Once back in Paris, Lavin called the lead baritone of the company and asked to see him. They met for coffee in a café near Lavin's office. He had seen Coudert as a man of experience, not only in the opera but in life. He had three suspects: Adelaide Aubin, Adam Basset, and perhaps Andre Piquet, who might have sought to avenge his sister. But he did not consider any of them as strong suspects. In particular, Piquet was in Aix, far from the Loire. But he had once been an actor and could have posed as a waiter at the inn. This seemed far-fetched however.

Lavin asked Coudert if he knew about Bergeron's brief career.

"Yes, We are a small community, and our lives are intertwined."

"What stood out about Bergeron aside from his talent?"

"He was temperamental and was a constant thorn in the side of his directors. He thought he knew how to play and sing the parts better than any of them."

"How did he get along with M. de France?"

"De France admired his talent and worked hard to teach Alain how to improve his singing, but Alain saw these efforts as criticism, and he resisted. He sang very well, but he would have improved if he had listened to the director."

"How did de France respond?"

"He did not give up, and it could lead to tension and conflict. I remember one rehearsal that had to be suspended until the two men had cooled off."

Lavin thanked him and placed a call to the manager of the company, Marcel Favre, asking for an appointment. The company's offices were modest but attractive in an old mansion in St. Germain.

Favre was a rotund man, balding, with a small moustache, and shrewd eyes. Lavin asked him if he had any thoughts about the murder of Bergeron.

"No, Inspector," said Favre. "I am in the dark. As you know, I was not on the retreat. I had expected to hear from you already."

"I should have called you before now," said Lavin, "but I have been busy with interviews. Can you tell me about any conflicts that Bergeron might have had within the company?"

Favre said nothing at first, and Lavin waited. "Well," said Favre, "perhaps you should know that Bergeron complained to me that he was not happy with de France's direction of the operas."

"Direction in general or just with Alain's roles?"

"He wanted me to fire de France."

"Would you have done that?"

"No. Bergeron would have left us before long because he was becoming a star. However, we were a stable base for him, so I might have let him go elsewhere from time to time and used Adam Basset and perhaps jobbed in another singer."

"Did you know that Bergeron got a manager removed from a production in another company?"

"I knew it and so did de France. He threatened to resign after the latest blow-up unless I cashiered Bergeron"

"So it was a stand-off? What were you going to do?"

"I did nothing, temporized. I did not want to lose either of them. I hoped that perhaps time would resolve things."

The inspector returned to Geoffrey Coudert, the baritone and asked, "Was there open conflict between Bergeron and de France during the retreat?"

"Yes. We were discussing the role of the Count in "The Barber of Seville," our first production in September. Alain wanted to play the role in a subtle and less robust way than de France wanted. They had a knock down and drag out fight before the entire company."

"Why did no one tell me this?"

"We are good, as a company, in smoothing over personal conflicts for the sake of our artistry."

Lavin then called the critic, Guy Dione, and asked what he knew about the personal history of Charles de France.

"He was a good but not great baritone. He took up directing early in his career."

"And before that?"

He studied music at a good conservatory."

"And before that?"

"I believe that he was in the army, as a conscript."

"Do you know what he did in the army?"

"No, but you can find the records to tell you."

It was not difficult to find that de France had been in a Special Forces unit in French Algieria to capture warlords and restore order. A discussion with a commander of such units informed the inspector that Special Forces soldiers were skillful with pistols, rifles, knives, and their bare hands if need be.

Lavin called de France and asked to see him. The director readily agreed.

When Lavin arrived at the office, the police were already there. He wondered how they could know his thoughts. Then a sergeant told him that de France had just shot himself thirty minutes ago. His secretary was sobbing.

Lavin asked her what had happened in the office that morning.

"Nothing, except a telephone call from M. Favre an hour ago."

Lavin did not need to inquire further. The mystery was solved. He went home early to see Sylvine.

Made in the USA
Columbia, SC
30 October 2017